INTIMACIES

INTIMACIES

Eleven More Stories

LUCY CALDWELL

faber

First published in 2021
by Faber & Faber Limited
Bloomsbury House, 74–77 Great Russell Street
London WC1B 3DA

Typeset by Typo•glyphix, Burton-on-Trent DE14 3HE
Printed and bound in the UK by CPI Group (UK) Ltd, Croydon CR0 4YY

'Like This' was commissioned and broadcast by BBC Radio 4
(October 2018); 'Mayday' was published in *The Glass Shore*, ed. Sinéad Gleeson
(New Island, 2016); 'Night Waking' was published in *Still Worlds Turning*,
ed. Emma Warnock (No Alibis Press, 2019); 'The Children' was published
in *Resist*, ed. Ra Page (Comma Press, 2019) and shortlisted for the
2019 BBC National Short Story Award.

A CIP record for this book
is available from the British Library

ISBN 978–0–571–353743

2 4 6 8 10 9 7 5 3 1

for Orla Rose
and all the places we, you, will go

And
always embrace things, people earth
sky stars, as I do, freely and with
the appropriate sense of space.

Frank O'Hara, 'A True Account of
Talking to the Sun at Fire Island'

Contents

INTIMACIES

Like This

IT HAPPENS LIKE THIS.

It's a Tuesday or Wednesday, one of those amorphous midweek days not quite the weekend, but at least not Monday. November. Grey rain coming down too vertically to pretend much longer, to yourself or anyone else, that it isn't really raining; impossible to cadge a minute's interest longer in the sad-mouthed, slightly ragged goldfish in the shallow ornamental pond. The pond is opposite a corporate law firm with a Dickensian name and persistent rumours of being built on Europe's largest medieval charnel house. There is a Perspex floor that you can walk or crawl over, peering giddily down to where old Roman walls and bronze-cast statues lie. The layers beneath; the bones. The fish and the floor are usually enough to kill half an hour; there is sometimes a bus too, an old red double-decker, repurposed into a puppet theatre, but not today.

You're running out of ideas.

The toddler is grizzling, the baby is grizzling. Any moment now one or both of them will go nuclear. You lift the flap on the rain hood and reach in to stroke the baby's soft damp cheek and she turns her head and blindly rootles, trying to suck your fingers. You fed her before you left the house, less than an hour ago. She can't be hungry. Unless she's due a new growth spurt – how old is she again?

Poor second-born. You counted her brother's age religiously, days, weeks, months, until the months flipped more pragmatically into years. But you've lost count already of how many weeks the baby is. Twelve, you think, or maybe thirteen? First time round you agonised, laughed in disbelief, joked grimly, about the tiredness. This time there isn't the energy even for that.

'You're hungry,' you say. 'Poor wee thing, you're hungry.'

'And I,' your toddler says indignantly. 'I hungry too. Naughty Mummy,' he adds, because you forgot to refill the snack box before leaving home. All it contained when you snapped it open was a long-suffering banana, blackened and bumped and rejected with affront, and some crumbs of rice cake currently disintegrating in the law firm's pond.

So although you can't justify it now you're a family of four on one salary and a maternity pittance, into Frankie's in the covered market it is; one of the few places round here likely to be vaguely tolerant of little boys and babies, even in combination, at least until the lunch rush starts, for normal people who don't eat lunch at 11.17.

Into Frankie's, order at the counter, today's lotto of foods that will or won't be eaten, choosing a table, wrestling with a stack of recalcitrant highchairs, highchair rejected, menu,

2

crayons, layers of nursing vests and stubborn clips of nursing bras and the howling baby finally latched on. Cutting up food left-handed, coaxing aeroplane mouthfuls in, baby breaking off and crying, burping baby, switching her sides, broken crayons, one more mouthful, sorry-I-mean-cargoplane, into the hangar. Transferring baby to buggy, easing her down, coaxing the straps over her shoulders (why didn't we get a buggy with a proper bassinet) and clicking them tight. Now finally your cup of tea, still warm because they make it with bloody steam—

'I need a wee-wee,' your toddler says.

You turn to him helplessly. The disabled toilet is out of order again, you can see the yellow sign on the door from here. The unisex loos aren't wide enough for the buggy and if you take the baby out now, she'll wake and howl, you'll have to feed her back to sleep, and she'll be sick because she's already gorged herself milk-drunk.

'I need a wee-wee now,' he says.

'Ok,' you say. 'Hang on.'

'*Mummy!*' he shouts in anguish. 'It's popping out so fast!'

'Go,' the woman beside you says. 'I'll keep an eye on the pram. Just go.'

'Are you sure?' you say gratefully, already reaching for your toddler's hand, 'thank you so much, thank you,' and you're hurrying with him to the toilets, and there, it's already happened, just like that, not even a second's split shiver of thought.

You have exchanged polite, distracted snatches of conversation with this woman, it should be said. In the midst of your caravanserai of chaos, she's commented on the baby, said hello to the toddler and asked him what he's drawing. Good on you for breastfeeding. Best start for them, no doubt about it. I couldn't stick to it with mine. An obvious cue that you politely took up: Oh, you have children too? Oh, long grown up now. A boy and a girl. Just like you. It flies by. Really? Believe you me. It doesn't feel that way in the trenches, but yes, it does. I'll take your word for it.

It hits you while you're in the cubicle, bent holding him, back aching, over the too-tall toilet because he refuses to sit down, insists that boys wee standing up. You have left the most helpless, precious thing you own with a complete and utter stranger.

No, you tell yourself. No. She has children too. She said so. And then you think: You don't even know the first thing about her. Of course you'd *say* you have kids. That's the first thing you'd say. And why was she so keen to strike up conversation with an obviously harassed and beleaguered new mum, so quick to insist that you leave her with the buggy?

'Hurry up,' you snarl at your son. You couldn't even say what the woman looked like now. Brownish hair, and glasses – did she have glasses? Fifty, sixty? Wearing something . . . dark? You yank up your son's pants and trousers, bundle him out through the cubicle door and past the sinks.

'But, Mummy!' He is outraged. 'I hasn't washed my *hands*. You has to wash your hands. You has to!'

4

'Not this time,' you snap, 'come *on*,' and you haul the protesting mass of him through the door.

Your heart, slamming into your chest.

The buggy is still there.

For a moment, your limbs turn to jelly. You clutch your toddler's hand and steady yourself on the metal edge of someone else's table. The buggy is still there. The beating wing of some great, ancient, thwarted creature brushes past and through you. Sick with relief, you kneel and hug your son.

'Mummy's sorry, sweetheart. Mummy didn't mean to be cross.'

He blinks at you, unsure, uneasy, this little barometer of your every mood and thought, disturbed and confused by the sudden rush of conflicting pressures.

'I am *very* cross,' he says. 'I am crosser than you. You *has* to wash your hands.' His face like thunder, little chin still jutting out in the ominous way that precedes a meltdown.

'I know,' you say, 'I know, pet, Mummy's sorry, Mummy's very sorry. Let's get your baby sister and then would you like a cookie? Or a milkshake? Which would you rather, a milkshake or a cookie?'

He glares, suspicious.

'A milkshake *and* a cookie,' he says.

'Ok,' you say, 'a milkshake and a cookie.'

'A stawby milkshake,' he says, sensing the upper hand, and you're suddenly overcome with love for him, this two-foot tyrant who can't yet pronounce 'strawberry'.

'A strawberry milkshake, of course. Come on.'

You weave back through the tables to thank the woman. You can't see her, at first, in the early-lunchtime throng, a queue for the counter that snakes past your table. Excuse me. Excuse me, please. Your son chiming in: Beep-beep! The muslin draped over the buggy hood to shade the sleeping baby has fallen to the floor. Almost before you have registered it something shivers through you. Those wings again, not defeated after all, not even retreating, just turning to make a closer circle, slow ripples in the air.

They never find the woman, or the baby. CCTV, *Newsnight*, the front page of the *Evening Standard*: nothing. Friends and well-meaning strangers say, It's not your fault, or, It could have happened to anyone, but of course it is, and of course it couldn't, wouldn't. The policewoman at the station: I'm sorry, just to clarify, she was a stranger to you? A complete stranger? Someone you'd never seen or spoken to before?

Your sweet, sweet baby, and the cluster of things you know about her. Her hands still in fists, and the way she'd started to laugh. The cracked, tender patches on her feet and elbows where you nightly rubbed in emollient. The way it felt to lay the warm soft bundle of her down in her Moses basket, bottom first, then gently lolling head. The way she gazed in wonder at the mobile of aeroplanes above her changing mat. The nights after vaccinations where her temperature rose and her little body twitched and trembled and you held her, rocked her, bounced her.

Her Babygro with the flamingos on, and her little vest with dinosaurs. A tiny hand on your chest as she fed. Still, nightly, year after year after year, your body aches for her.

The years slip by. They are three and one, and chasing each other through the glittering fountains in a park. They are four and two and feeding the swans, eating oversized ice creams side by side. They are seven and five, on a trampoline. Eight and six, nine and eleven. Twelve, thirteen, fourteen, teenagers, allies and enemies, officially adults, going, going, gone.

The marriage doesn't survive, or rather, it does until the new baby's born and you feel too guilty and wracked with anxiety to hold it, let alone risk loving it. Your husband goes for full custody of both and you don't fight it. You stay together for the sake of the boy, but separate by mutual agreement once he turns eighteen, and of course you never have another baby. He doesn't remember his baby sister at all, though he sometimes pretends he does.

'Mummy,' your son says. '*Mummy*,' tugging on your hand.

'My baby,' you say, to the cafe in general. 'Have you seen my baby?'

Asking. In general and at random, too loud at first and then even louder. My baby, have you seen my baby.

Some faces look at you, cease talking, wary, blank.

'Your mother took her,' someone says.

'My mother,' you say. Your mother. Your mother is across the water, hundreds of miles away.

'No,' you say, 'no, no, my mother's not here, she's not my mother, where did she go, did you see her, where did she go?'

The faces, blank.

'Just over there, I think?' The direction of the doors.

The mass of people: faces, talking. Dark jackets everywhere, brownish hair. A teenager, spots still on her cheeks, wearing the Frankie's baseball cap and badge.

'Excuse me, can I help you?'

'She's lost her mother.'

'She's not her mother.'

And suddenly you can no longer speak, and suddenly: there she is. Wearing a navy jacket and jeans, tortoiseshell glasses – yes – and a bright silk scarf knotted round her neck (how could you have missed the scarf?). Grey-brown hair in a bob, jiggling the baby in her arms.

Your baby.

'We woke up,' she says, 'didn't we? We woke up, so we went for a little walk, yes we did.'

'Is everything ok?' the Frankie's girl says, looking between you, as you scoop the baby back into your arms. And *oh*, the warm heft of her, this is how she feels, *this*. The soft downy hair on her head, her neck, the milky smell of her, this.

'Everything's good?' the Frankie's girl says again.

'She never wakes up,' you say.

The woman blinks at you.

'She never wakes up,' you say, feeling the pitch of your voice rising. 'Once she's fed and asleep like that, she never wakes up unless she's disturbed.'

8

Like This

'Well, she woke up,' the woman says, 'and I didn't want to leave her crying, so I lifted her.'

Trudging home, drenched, unwieldy buggy-board bumping down and up the slick kerbs, already the thought of anything other than this, implausible. The veil between worlds, the skin closing over. A wanderer who visits another world and spends a lifetime there, only to return to their own and not a minute passed. Just wanting this day to end now, that moment when, the children bathed, tucked into bed or zipped and poppered into duvet bag, flush-cheeked and open-mouthed, asleep and peaceful, you exhale.

It's only just beginning.

Mayday

TEN DAYS LATER, THE PACKAGE FINALLY COMES. It is a small brown padded envelope, her name and address typed on a white label. The postmark is the Netherlands. Inside is a blister pack of tablets, one round and four oval. No instructions, no warnings, and nothing to identify the sender. She pops out the round tablet there and then, in the hallway, and tries to swallow it down but her mouth is too dry. She feels it stuck at the back of her throat. She makes it into the kitchen and pours a pint glass of water, drinks the whole thing down. The glass has a dried scum of lace at its neck and the water tastes stale. She can still feel the sensation of the tablet, lodged. There was a fresher, a geography student, who died after taking diet pills that he bought online. Boiled alive: that's what the newspapers said. There was a photo of him in his hospital bed, face so swollen he appeared to have no eyes, the skin on his torso and arms peeling off in raw red patches the size of sycamore leaves. His parents had released it as a warning, a deterrent to others.

It is the last day of April and she has, by repeated calculations, less than one week remaining.

Mayday

A memory: aged eleven, a Junior Strings weekend away in Carnlough. On Sunday morning the Catholic children go to Mass in the big church on the Bay Road; the handful of Protestants are supposed to stay in Drumalla House and sing hymns with the cello teacher. She goes with the Catholics: the walk along the rocky shore, the sweet shop in the village afterwards. The sense of something forbidden. Her friends line up to receive Holy Communion and she copies them, kneels and opens her mouth and lets the priest place the dry disc of wafer on her tongue. She chews, swallows. Afterwards they tell her she's going to Hell. They are falling over themselves to tell her. She's committed a Mortal Sin, and because she can't go to Confession she can't be forgiven. And she *chewed*. They are beside themselves with glee. She cries. The cello teacher tells her it's nonsense, tells the others they're being silly. Tells them that, incidentally, the word used in John Chapter 6 to describe the consumption of the Eucharist can be understood as 'to gnaw' or 'to munch', so there they go, and now enough of all that. They say they were only joking.

She hasn't thought of it for years but it surfaces now. The dusty room they practised in, the bars of sunlight. The pebbles on that little rocky shore. The gules of light in the stained-glass windows of the Catholic church.

She doesn't know what to do with herself now, with the hours remaining. She checks her phone. 11.11.Tomorrow, at this time exactly, the other pills, all four of them at once. It would still be possible, if she hurried, to make the midday seminar. But she hasn't been to lectures all week, hasn't done the seminar prep. She likes the module, likes the tutor, wants to do well. Last term her supervisor said her idea had PhD potential and she replayed the words in her head for weeks. So she goes up to her room now and sits at her desk and flips through the handout and reading lists. *Gender, Family, Faith: Norms and Controversies. Paradise Lost in Context. Civil Wars of Ideas: Politics vs. Religion.* You can't get away from religion, in the seventeenth century. She reaches for the Norton anthology, opens it at random. A ballad. She skims the first couple of stanzas:

> Farewell, rewards and fairies,
> Good housewives now may say,
> For now sluts in the dairies
> Do fare as well as they.

> Lament, lament, old abbeys
> The fairies lost command;
> They did but change priests' babies,
> But some have changed your land.

> And all your children stolen from thence
> Who live as changelings ever since

She stops, heart pounding. Sluts. Illegitimate children. Changelings, and fairies to blame them upon. Nothing feels neutral any more, she thinks. It never will again.

And then: Wise up, she tells herself, and then she says it aloud. Wise up. Wise yer bap: that's what they used to say in school. Wise yer bap. She forces herself to tap her laptop awake and type out a few lines of the ballad. It's going to be fine. It's all going to be fine.

She closes her laptop and lies down on her bed, scans her body for any signs it's starting to feel different. What if nothing happens? What if it *is* too late? The thing is, you find out and you think, ok, nine weeks, that's ages. But then you do the online calculator and realise with a horrible rush that it's already more than six weeks, coming up to seven. It doesn't feel fair, the way they count it. Nine weeks is nothing. Nine weeks gives you little more than a fort-night. She found the website that night, Sunday, and by the Tuesday had made up her mind and placed the order. But it still might be too late. If she hadn't found out until a few days later. Or if it had happened while she still lived at home, or before she had a credit card or a PayPal account. It doesn't bear thinking about but the thoughts keep marching back, a fortnight's well-worn grooves. If you were in England, the GP would have prescribed it to you, the exact same thing. You'd have taken it already, under medical supervision. It would already be over. If this doesn't work she still has options. London, or Manchester: she's researched the clinics online. She wonders will she tell her mum, if it comes to that. Her mum would make the appointments, book the flights, pay for the hotel. Hold her hand in the waiting room and hug her afterwards. Her mum wouldn't rage at her, or weep, like mothers do in films. Her mum would be pragmatic, calm: her mum would handle it all. Why hasn't she told her mum? Her mum has raised the three of them to believe that they can do whatever they want, that they're as good as men, that it's a woman's right to choose. Her mum would help her. Her mum would be here, now.

She aches for her.

Another memory: the Junior Debating Club, fourth year or maybe fifth. Kerry Ferguson passing round A4 pictures of babies smiling in the womb, sucking their thumbs. The women should just have them, Kerry Ferguson says. They should have them and give them to people who want them. Almost nobody voted For. Afterwards, when her mum asks how her day was, she's too ashamed to mention it.

The day passes slowly, seeps into evening. The sky through her rooflight window is high and pale. The sounds of her housemates coming in, the clatter of pans, the smells of cooking. Someone smoking in the yard; the smell of it turning her stomach. Is anything happening yet? Eat and drink as normal, the website says, avoiding alcohol in case it skews your judgement. She hasn't felt hungry all day, has eaten just granola bars, handfuls of Crunchy Nut Corn Flakes. One of her housemates taps on her door. Is she ok? Yeah, fine, she says, period cramps. Oh God, poor you, I've Nurofen if you want? Nah, thanks a million but I've got some here. Fair do's. Here, we're going for a pint in a bit if you feel any better. Thanks, I reckon I'll just stay here, though, watch something. Ok, cool, give us a shout sure if you need anything. Cool, seeya. Bye.

The sky is streaked with pink now. Her phone beeps with a text from her mum: her grandma has been taken to the Ulster again, another chest infection. Every time it happens they think it's going to be it this time, but it somehow never is, and after a five-day course of antibiotics Grandma's discharged back to the nursing home to lie corroding in her rubber-sheeted bed. She can't think what to text back. Does her mum mean she should visit? She can't set foot in a hospital: what if it started happening there, in front of all the nurses and doctors? (If there are complications and you have to go to hospital, don't tell them. They can't tell, and they don't have to know. The treatment in any case will be the same. No tests can prove what you've taken, what you've done.) She starts to reply, deletes it. Her phone beeps again. *Don't mean to alarm you,* her mum says, *it's the same sad old story, just thought you'd want to know.* A string of x's and o's. Then a third message: *Are you back for Sunday lunch?*

She blinks. Sunday. Sunday lunch. *Hope so*, she replies, then, *Sorry, in middle of essay crisis. Sorry to hear about Grandma.*

Dad's with her now, her mum says. *It's just so very sad, isn't it. Poor Dad.*

I'll text him, she says.

A few minutes later her mum sends another text: *Good luck with essay!* followed by a fountain pen emoji, some books, a cup of coffee and a hamster head. Then another text: *Sorry! That was meant to be a lucky cat. Need my glasses!*

An evening from her childhood: this time of year, these lingering days and pale, light skies. Their dad has asked their mum to call in on their grandma the odd time during the week and one night after swimming they do. They scramble out of the car and race across the green then stop, for reasons they can't put into words, and wait. A chill wind is coming from the lough, cutting straight through their uniforms, green pinafores and blue summer blouses. Their hair scorched dry on top but still damp at the nape of their necks, the sharp, clean smell of chlorine on their skin. Their mum reaches them, takes her youngest sister's hand. The pebble-dashed terrace of houses, each with its doll's-house gate, impeccable roses or trimmed box-hedge borders. Beyond them the garages, beyond that the forest. It's not really a forest, though they call it that, just a close-growing cluster of larch trees at the back of the estate. The fallen needles make the ground feel soft and springy and not like ground at all. They absorb all sound too, the road on one side, the estate on the other, so that as soon as you're through the first row of trees you could be miles or years from anywhere. But now their grandma's face is looming pinkly in the bubbled glass beside the door, and the door opens inwards, not enough to let them in. Their grandma touching her hair: What's this, now, is something the matter?

Her minister is there; he's stopped by after the Mothers' Union. There are slices of buttered fruit loaf on the table nest as well as a plate of oatmeal biscuits. The electric heater is pulled out to the centre of the room, its face aglow with all three bars. The minister stands, greets their mum, then all of them by name. The Reverend knows you from the photographs, their grandma says, and touches her hair again, straightens her blouse. Her youngest sister steps forward, pirouettes. Do you like our new hair? They've all had it cut for the summer term, from almost waist-length to bobs, because of nits – but he doesn't need to know that, they see the warning in their mum's eye. They all shake their heads to show how it swishes. The Reverend says, Vanity, vanity, and their grandma laughs, but his face is serious. Vanity, vanity! he says again. Vanity in young ladies is a terrible thing to behold, for it takes deep root, and what grows crooked cannot be straightened. Their grandma looks at him and stops smiling, and after that she won't admire their haircuts or even meet their eyes, and they are confused and when they leave their mum is furious.

His face was red and his hair was white and his eyes were bright blue. He's dead now, and soon Grandma will be, whether or not it happens this time. The larch trees are gone too, lopped down to stumps.

She makes herself remember, instead, those Tuesday swimming lessons at Olympia. Imagines watching afterwards, through the observation window in the second-floor cafeteria, the lane ropes being dragged into place and the club swimmers powering up and down in their powder-blue caps, flipping into easy tumbleturns, length, after length, after length.

Her housemates go out. She texted him twice, then a third time. He didn't reply. Her phone said the messages had been delivered and once she even saw the *dot, dot, dot* of him composing a reply but then the dots went away and the reply never came. She saw him a week later in the Clements in Botanic and he was obviously scundered, said he'd lost his phone and only just got a new one. Give us your number, sure, he said, and she did, but she knew he wouldn't contact her and he didn't. After that she could hardly tell him – could she? – why she'd been trying to get in touch. It should be his problem too, but it just isn't, the world doesn't work like that. So he'll never know any of this. He'll never even suspect. For a strange moment, she feels almost sorry for him. Something about that makes a sort of sense in the middle of the night. But when she wakes, the feeling is gone.

Mayday

She can't be in the house. She walks into town but it's too early for the shops to be open and then it starts to rain, heavy and dull. Yesterday's light, high skies have closed right down, thick cloud and raw, damp air. It is the first of May. Mayday, she thinks. She remembers from Guides that you have to say it three times in a row. Mayday mayday. She goes back. Two of her housemates are up, both hungover, smoking in the kitchen. She makes a cup of tea, sits with them a bit. Talks; hears herself talk. Laughs. Tells them about the Sunday in Carnlough, the Holy Communion. They all laugh about it. She goes up to her room. At 11.11 she takes the second lot of pills: all four of them. They're chalky and bitter under her tongue. At 11.21 they've hardly dissolved at all. Her jaw aches with the effort of holding her mouth and tongue still. She gives it until 11.25, watching the minutes pass on her phone. Then 11.30. That has to be enough. She swallows what remains of them down with some water from her bottle. She can't go out again now. It is likely to start working within two hours but may take up to five, or in some cases even longer. She opens her laptop and goes to the website, checks to see if there's anything she's missed. Then deletes her browsing history again: clear history, reset top sites, remove all website data.

She waits for the guilt to start, the regret, but it doesn't. What does she feel? She tests out emotions. Scared, yes. Definitely scared. She's deleted her browsing history seventeen, eighteen times. But they have ways of finding these things out, and somewhere, etched onto the internet, is her name, her address, her PayPal account: what she did. When, where and how. She, or anyone who helps her, could be jailed for life. So, scared. What else does she feel? Sadness. She wants to have babies one day. She wants to see the blue line and feel giddy with excitement, check its weekly growth. She wants to want it. But not like this. The other thing she feels, to her surprise, is relief. An overwhelming, incredible sense of relief: that she is doing the right thing.

When the bleeding comes, the first dull smear on toilet paper, and then the first, warm drops, she will be so relieved (and sad, and scared) all over again that she will cry. She's bought maxi-pads instead of her usual Lil-Lets and the trickling feeling between her thighs will make her think of her first-ever period, of climbing into her mother's lap and feeling too big to be there, sobbing. Everything that is irrevocable now: all that has been lost. You mustn't think like that. She will remind herself: the bleeding and cramps are likely to be worse than a normal period, and there may be clots. Light bleeding may continue for up to three weeks. In most cases, four to six weeks after bleeding stops, your period will resume. She will recite it to herself, over and over again, like a litany, a prayer. She will be one of the lucky ones. She will. She will.

People Tell You Everything

IN A TINY BASEMENT COCKTAIL BAR AROUND THE CORNER
from the office, I was having drinks with Rachel Work.
They were technically birthday drinks, though she didn't
know that, and wouldn't, unless I got drunk and blurted it
out, which I was hoping I didn't, because that would just
be weird.

I also had to remember to call her *Rachel* or *Rach* and not
Rachel Work, which she was saved as in my phone. I didn't
know her full name – the office had an email system that
only used first names, and on the website it just had first
names too. *Rachel, Ben, Dmitri, Alex, Paola*, each with a
quirky photograph, white-water rafting or hula-hooping or
face-painted at a music festival. Rachel's was at a masked
ball, or maybe a Secret Cinema, holding up a gold eye mask
with plumed red feathers and blowing a fake, extravagant
kiss through pillar-box lips to whoever was taking the picture. The photo was entirely not like Rachel, or at least the
Rachel Work I knew, which I supposed was maybe the
point – we were a creative brand agency, after all.

The second cocktail, Rachel was saying, had not been as

good as the first. 'Sorry, the online reviews of this place looked really good. Maybe I'm getting too old for Shoreditch,' she said, and we both laughed, though it crossed my mind that I didn't actually know how old she was: five years older than me, ten? Her hair was in an asymmetric platinum bob and behind her square black glasses her eyes were crinkled, though that could have been because she laughed a lot.

'Well, here's to getting too old for Shoreditch,' I said, and we clinked glasses and downed what remained of the gin-whatevers she'd chosen.

It's your birthday, I told myself, but it's going to be fine. It's not an important one. It's just another day. I was seeing some uni friends for drinks on Saturday; my mum and dad and grandma had sent me cards. My mum had also sent me a skirt from Gap four sizes too big, because she'd remembered they did American sizes you had to either add or subtract two from, and gotten it the wrong way round. I almost told Rachel this, for something else to laugh about, until I remembered I couldn't.

I set my glass down.

'Shall we give them one last chance?' said Rachel.

'Why not!' I said, and she went up to order.

My phone had buzzed in my pocket several minutes ago, and I'd been concentrating on not thinking about it. It would be him, I thought. Finally, finally, it would be him – except it wasn't, of course, it was just my brother.

Happy birthday!! Conall had written, with a picture of him and David grinning, faces smushed together, holding up champagne flutes.

You guys! I texted back, with a string of champagne-bottle and heart emojis.

It's all your fault, Conall messaged back immediately, with a winking face.

It was their anniversary today they'd got together on my twenty-first, which had been a last-minute, very drunken house party thrown by my then-flatmates, horrified I'd nothing better planned, because unlike people back home, for whom it was all about your eighteenth, English people made a big deal of their twenty-firsts. They'd texted round everyone they could think of who might be free on a random Monday in May, and luckily for Conall, David had been one of those people.

And now here we were, another May Monday, and it could happen, my mum, who suspected something, but didn't know anything, kept telling me. One of these days, you could just meet the love of your life.

I watched Rachel at the bar, intent on communicating something to the barman, gesticulating at the menu, until he held his hands up and out: I surrender, you win.

He tossed and caught the bottle of spirits on his forearm, poured it into the cocktail shaker from a height, then flipped and spun the shaker, and winked. Rachel shook her head at him and laughed.

I suddenly just wanted to get the rest of the evening over with. As soon as it was done and he hadn't texted, I'd know for sure he wasn't going to.

I was at the agency on maternity cover, the longest stretch of work I'd managed to find since leaving the oral history archive so abruptly. They were a young and growing consultancy, and if I played my cards right, or at least didn't play them wrong, it might lead to a full-time position. That was the plan, or so I said to my mum. We *created a sense of belonging for vibrant hospitality ventures*, we *captured confidence in change*, we *engaged people with actionable brand experiences*. Making up stories; clouds of obscuring words. It was the opposite of the work at the archive, where we'd listen meticulously, transcribing and notating every hesitation, every pause, every stumble and even inaccuracy. It was the opposite of my master's thesis too, which had been on certainties and uncertainties in the works of Szymborska and Miłosz, and for which, as I spoke no Polish, I'd combed through reams of translations, the myriad possibilities opened up by each choice of word.

I had never been able to explain, to my bemused parents, or even to my friends, why I'd chosen to write on poets whose language I didn't speak, from a place I'd never been. Maybe I couldn't have explained it even to myself. And then, for a while, it had all made a sort of sense. I'd clung to that, when things seemed impossible, when my friends told me I was stupid, then ran out of ways of telling me.

Oh, the slamming relief when a text or an email would flash up with his name.

Two years of my life. A job I'd loved.

Twenty-seven.

My best friend from uni, who was into tarot and astrological charts these days, said twenty-seven was the age of our Saturn Return. Your Saturn Return was when transiting Saturn was finally conjunct again with your natal chart. It meant your chickens came home to roost. You were a kid no longer. Apparently, how you dealt with it set the tone for the rest of your life. Or something. Maybe, I thought, I should just leave London. Move back home. But every time I thought of it, I thought of stepping off the plane under a grey and muffled sky, into the bowl of the hills; the particular smell of my parents' house that never failed to set off an inexplicable ache inside me, as if I'd yet again come in from school to the smell of onions frying or potatoes on the boil, wet leaves and crushed beechnuts on the mat in the back porch and homework to do; and I thought of my school friends with their buggies in Belmont Park, their neat Corsas and Peugeots with *Baby on Board!* stickers, and it felt already all too late.

'Cheers, babe,' said Rachel, coming back with the new drinks, and I tried to put some cheer into my reply. 'So this is an oolong martini,' she said. 'It's made with a Taiwanese milk oolong, crème de cacao, a silver mescal, and aquafaba instead of egg-white. What do you reckon?'

I took a sip of the frothy top. Despite the list of ingredients, it wasn't actually bad.

'Yeah!' I said. 'Yeah, no, it's good!'

She beamed.

'He insisted it needed egg-white,' she said, 'but, hello, vegan? So I told him to make it with aquafaba, only not to shake it too much, or it'd go viscous.'

'Are you vegan?' I said. 'I didn't know you were vegan.'

'Course you did!' she said. I thought of our lunches, sitting on the bench by the eucalyptus tree. My Tupperware with whatever leftover pasta I'd thrown in, or a default cheese-and-cucumber bap, and the elaborate salads she'd insist on sharing with me, sweet potato and home-made beetroot dip and pomegranate molasses. The coconut-milk cappuccino she'd always get from the posh coffee place, versus my milky Americano or regular flat white.

'Oh yeah,' I said, 'I suppose I did,' and she laughed.

We both sipped at our drinks. We'd cycled through our limited repertoire of work jokes and now we were flailing, even with the oolong martinis' help.

'So, you're running the Berlin Marathon,' I said, although we'd already covered that when Rachel said these would be her last drinks for a while, with training in earnest beginning next week. 'I will definitely sponsor you. Just sign me up.'

'Babe – why don't you do it too?' she said. 'Alex is doing it, and I think Dmitri. We could all train together – it'd be a laugh.'

'No offence, but I actually couldn't hate running more,' I said, and she threw her head back and laughed.

'Seriously,' I said, 'I still get post-traumatic flashbacks of forced cross-country around Cairnburn in the rain.'

'Your accent's stronger when you talk about home,' she said.

'Is it?'

'Yeah, it totally is.'

'Oh right,' I said, and tried, and failed, to think of something funny to say. 'My inner millie,' I eventually managed, and she smiled and shook her head.

'I didn't catch that, babe – your inner what?'

I didn't have the energy. 'It's nothing,' I said.

'No, seriously, I love all your "wee" Belfast phrases. What was it you said the other day? Oh yeah – "Who all's going" somewhere. I love that. "Who all's going". I'd love to go to Belfast,' she said. 'Maybe you'll take me one day.'

'Ha,' I said, 'maybe.'

There was another silence.

'I'm sorry,' I said. 'It's just—'

'It's ok, hun,' said Rachel, and gave my hand a squeeze.

I felt hot, treacherous tears well up in my eyes.

'You can tell me anything,' she said.

I had an email saved in my Drafts folder, written to my future self. I'd written it last Christmas Eve – or, I supposed, technically, Christmas Day. He had promised that after Christmas he was going to tell her everything, and end it. He just wanted to get Christmas over with first. They'd flown back to Wrocław on the twenty-first, and the following day I'd come to Belfast, and although it was just four days, or really only three, that I hadn't heard from him, those flights, that distance, made everything seem far longer.

In Poland, it was all about Christmas Eve. On Christmas Eve afternoon, you decorated your Christmas tree, and

27

when you saw *Gwiazdka*, the little star, the first star of evening, you lit the tree's lights and Christmas had begun. Then you sat down with your extended family to a meal with twelve dishes, the centrepiece a whole carp. After dinner, you exchanged gifts, and went to midnight Mass. The next day, Christmas Day, was a public holiday, but there was nothing particularly special about it: it was more like our Boxing Day.

It had always been about Christmas Eve for me too – about the build-up, the anticipation, the house full of secrets, the drawing-in – and I was sure that he'd find a moment to write to me, *Happy Christmas Eve*, even if that was all it said. I looked up the time of sunset in Wrocław: twilight began at twelve minutes to four, which is when his nieces and nephews would be clamouring to spot the star, and be the one to announce that Christmas had begun, and I knew that's when he'd write.

I'd been into the city centre that morning, the last-minute messages my mother needed, posh cheese and biscuits for the neighbours coming round, extra rolls of wrapping paper. It was nothing I couldn't have got on the local high street, but I loved the almost-empty bus into town then walking the Christmas Eve streets, the knot of goths in front of the City Hall refusing to concede to the festive season, the cigarette-lighter men of my childhood, now that people hadn't the need of five lighters for a pound, selling flashing Santa hats and antlers and bristling strings of tinsel instead. The birch trees on Donegall Place, slender and bare, drawn up in the clear air, waiting. Into Corn Market, where the bandstand used to be, and the ravaged old man with his megaphone and placards, impossible to tell if the end he was proclaiming was *nigh* or *now*. The sky that Christmas Eve morning was pale, the hills iron-grey with cold, the city ingathered. Seagulls in from the lough, wheeling in circles, landing on lamp-posts and folding and unfolding their disdainful wings, the sense that despite themselves they were restlessly waiting too.

There was a hidden river running the length of High Street that once you knew about you couldn't help but feel underfoot, the eastward tug of it, and I always ended my walk by following its path past the Albert Clock and into Custom House Square, where its culverts met the Lagan. But before looping back on myself and heading for the bus stop home, I'd paused to listen to a group of carol singers outside the Mayfair Buildings, and as they sang the first tremulous lines of 'O Little Town of Bethlehem', the feeling of everything just about to happen built and built until I almost couldn't bear it any longer.

He'd never been to Belfast – not properly, at least. He'd flown in to do the *Game of Thrones* tour on a mate's stag do, and it had rained. He'd told me that, rolling his eyes and laughing, and although I'd usually be the first to criticise the place, how provincial it could be, how I couldn't wait to get away, I'd felt it like a punch to the gut.

Belfast didn't feel like mine exactly, any more, now I'd been gone so many years – I couldn't have told you where the best bars were, and the bus routes had all changed – but it still felt like a part of me: and how badly I wanted him, then, not in an abstract sense, or in some nebulous future, but right there beside me, Corn Market, Christmas Eve. I wanted him to see the city, to walk its streets with me, and I thought: I have to tell you this.

As the carol singers paused to shuffle their sheets, I took out my phone and wrote the beginnings of a haphazard, tumbling email that I'd continue all day, on the bus back home, in front of the fire and my family's traditional *It's A Wonderful Life*, as twelve minutes to four came and went, and on into the evening as Conall and David bickered in jest over how best to make Irish coffees, then later on in my single bed, my old childhood stocking hung on the doorknob. But as the night crept on and I didn't hear from him, didn't hear from him, I held back from sending it. As Christmas Eve tipped into Christmas Day, 00.00, 00.01, I wrote, instead, to myself; a message to be read when the moment finally came, when I needed it most, or could pretend no longer.

It was kind of a relief to think I hadn't got there yet, and also just exhausting.

'So I think you might be ready,' said Rachel. 'Do you want to hear my theory?'

She'd been telling me about her theory for the last few days, without actually telling me what the theory was. If she ever wrote a self-help book, she said, it would make a fortune: the theory was simple, and perfect.

'Hit me with it!' I said.

'Ok,' she said, 'here goes.' She took a gulp of her drink and set her glass aside, then moved aside the tea light too.

'People,' she said, leaning in across the little table, 'tell you everything.'

I waited.

'That's it,' she said. 'People – tell you – everything.'

'People . . .' I said.

'Yes,' she said. 'Tell you everything. All you need to know. Right away. Without your even asking.'

'Ok,' I said.

'Just think about it. A time when you've met someone, for the first time, and think back to what they said. People will literally tell you what you need to hear. The whole relationship is already there. And you just need to choose to hear it.'

'Huh,' I said.

'You see?' she said, and she sat back, pleased.

'Hang on,' I said.

It had been my first week at the archive, but he wasn't there – there'd been some conference, something. On the Thursday evening the other three members of the team and I had gone to join him at Toynbee Hall, where there was a drinks reception that had spilled out into the courtyard. I'd scrounged a menthol from some random girl, then realised he was standing beside me, watching me smoke it. I'd asked if he wanted some, and he'd said –

I closed my eyes while I tried to get it right.

He'd said –

I shouldn't, I gave up a couple of years back.

31

Then he takes it from me and says, *Just a drag, then*, and something like *You're a bad influence*, or *I'm too easily led*.

'Penny for them, babe?' said Rachel.

I opened my eyes. The bar was suddenly loud and I wasn't sure if I felt drunk or just tired.

'I was testing it out,' I said. 'Trying to remember – exactly.'

'And?' she said.

'Yeah,' I said, 'I don't know. Maybe,' and I tried to make myself smile.

We'd discussed Szymborska and Miłosz, and he'd asked me, as everyone always did, why I'd chosen to write about Polish poets, when there were so many great Irish ones.

For once, I don't know why, I'd told the truth.

'I don't know,' I'd said. 'But maybe chance has been toying with me for years. Maybe,' I'd said, 'I have a Polish soul,' and I'd said it extravagantly, so that he could laugh if he wanted to, but he hadn't laughed.

'I think the Polish and the Irish might be soulmates,' he'd said, and we'd scrounged another cigarette and shared it, staying outside even when it began to rain.

'Do you remember what you said the first time we met?' said Rachel.

'Yeah,' I said, though in truth I did only vaguely. 'It was in the churchyard.'

'Yup,' she said.

I remembered that much. I think I'd been walking round, looking for somewhere to sit and eat lunch, but all the benches must have been occupied and the grass wet. I'd done a couple of circuits, then – that's right – I'd heard someone calling from near the eucalyptus tree.

'You said I could share your bench,' I said. 'You said, I recognise you, you're Paola's cover.'

'Yeah,' she said, smiling. 'And you sat down, and it had been raining earlier, and the eucalyptus leaves smelled all sweet and fresh, that way they do – and you breathed it in and threw out your arms and said, It smells so new, doesn't it, as if you really could begin again. And we clinked forks and said, To new beginnings.'

'Yeah,' I said. I'd been determined to make the agency work: to be outgoing, easygoing, to be a new and better version of me.

I felt suddenly and indescribably sad.

Rachel put out a hand and touched my cheek.

'Rach?' I said.

'You know your cheeks are flushed,' she said. She smoothed my growing-out fringe behind my ear and I didn't know what to say. She stroked my cheek again, upwards, with the backs of her fingers, then downwards with her fingertips. 'You look so beautiful, you know.'

My heart stopped in my chest, then started going at double the speed.

'Hang on,' I said, a sort of panic and revulsion rising, not at her, exactly, but at this, at all of this, at the mess I was making of everything.

'It's ok, babe,' she said, 'this is *Shoreditch*. No one gives a fuck.'

'No,' I said, 'no, it's not that,' and before I'd even finished saying it she'd seen it in my eyes.

'Oh,' she said, and took her hand away. Then, 'Seriously?' she said. 'Shit. Oh, *fuck*.'

'I'm sorry,' I said. 'Rachel, I'm sorry.'

'But, hang on,' she said, then she stopped and laughed and shook her head. 'Ok,' she said. 'Ok.'

'I didn't,' I said, 'I mean, I didn't mean to—'

'We've been,' she said, 'I mean, every lunchtime for the last, what, month?'

There was a long, horrible silence.

'Look,' she eventually said, and drained the last of her drink. 'Let's not say another word about it. This is on me.'

'Not at all,' I protested, feebly and insincerely, as she got up to pay.

The toilets were thin-rimmed metal bowls, without even seats. I slid down the wall divide and squatted there and wondered was I going to throw up.

Your Saturn Return, my best friend said, will seem to make you trail destruction in your wake. Like the opposite of Midas, everything you touch will turn to shit. My head was spinning. I tried to concentrate on breathing, and simultaneously ignoring the sharp tang of the bleachy, pissy air.

My phone buzzed in my pocket, then buzzed again. I closed my eyes, sent up some arrow of prayer to God, or Saturn, or whomever, and got it out.

Rachel Work
Come on babe

Rachel Work
You don't need to do this

Rachel Work
It's all gonna be ok

It wasn't him. It wasn't him, it wasn't him.

For a moment, I thought of dropping my phone right into the toilet, so no one could text me, or not-text me, ever again. Instead, in the blue light of the cubicle, I swiped away her messages and scrolled down to his name, our conversation.

Can I call you up by sheer force of longing? The answer was always *no*, but it didn't seem to stop me trying.

There were some days when – for no real reason at all, the angle of the sun, the cloudlessness of the sky – I'd be sure he'd message me. He'd say, *I've missed you so much, these last few months, I know now I just want to be with you.* I'd check my phone all day, until the evening, when it began to be clear I'd been wrong – but *how?* It just never made sense.

I need more time, he'd said. I need more time.

I'd been sure he'd text me today. My birthday, by some weird fluke, also happened to be what in Poland would be my *imieniny*: the celebration of the saint who shared my name. 'It's very special,' he'd told me when he first realised, 'it means you're very special,' and for a while I'd let myself believe him; or let myself believe, at least, that to him I might be.

People tell you everything. Maybe they did, maybe they didn't. Maybe they already had, or maybe they never would. I scrolled up, up, through our conversation. *Even the birds are in the know*, he'd written, *I saw them writing in the sky / brazenly and openly / the very name I call you by.* *Beautiful*, I'd written, inanely. I scrolled back down.

The messaging service told you when someone was online, and when they were typing. Twice, after I'd ended things and quit the archive, I'd seen him, *typing . . . typing . . .* and my whole body had been instantly liquid with relief and desire. But the messages never came. These days, though I tried to make myself not check, he was never even online any more.

You're not there, I thought intensely to my phone.

Then I thought: You never really have been.

The unexpected relief of that thought. It was weirdly freeing. I swiped the thread left and tapped on the menu. *Delete Chat*, I selected. Are you sure? my phone asked me. Did I not want to *Archive Instead? Delete Chat*, I tapped again, and then, just like that, it was gone.

Outside the toilets, Rachel was waiting for me. I thought for a split second about pretending not to see her.

'Oh God,' I said.

'Come on,' she said. 'Let's go.'

I followed her through the now-rammed bar and up the stairs and out into the Shoreditch evening, the litter and graffiti and the neon lights, the bicycle repair yard opposite turned into a bar by night, all fairy lights and bunting, the Airstream trailers in the vacant car park now street-food vans. Deckchairs outside bars on scrappy squares of AstroTurf. The intermittent plane trees, huge and blotchy and recently pollarded, so alien when you really looked at them, just starting to sprout green leaves again. And the sky: that mid-May deepening blue, almost but not dark yet.

'So,' she said.

'After what we think of as twilight,' I found myself saying, 'which is technically civil twilight, comes nautical then astronomical twilight. At certain latitudes and at certain times of year, and even here in London for a handful of weeks in May and June, because of the way the twilights overlap, there's actually no night, and this is one of those nights.'

'How drunk are you?' said Rachel.

'It's not that,' I said. 'I mean, yes, I am quite, but that's not it. I just . . .' I said, and I knew I owed her an explanation, but I couldn't bring myself to say it. It wasn't even that she'd pity me, or think I was naive: I just couldn't risk it getting round the agency, that I'd left my previous job after an affair with the married boss.

We were all clichés, really, when you zoomed out enough. That's what my best friend and I used to say, before we sort of stopped talking.

That ache at the back of my throat. That constant, grinding loneliness.

'I just—' I said again.

'No, listen,' said Rachel. 'It's all on me. I somehow –
must have . . .' She stopped. 'Look, I'm sorry,' she said.

'No,' I said. 'Honestly.'

We stood and watched the Shoreditch evening go by.
The couples, the gaggles of girls arm-in-arm, or arm-in-
arm-in-arm, stumbling along and occasionally into the
road, where swarms of Deliveroo mopeds swerved and
beeped. A homeless man was making his way down the
road with a three-legged dog on a piece of rope, holding
out a disposable cup, and generally being ignored. When
he reached us, Rachel opened her wallet and took out a
tenner.

'Here you go, mate,' she said.

'Thank you,' he said. 'Thank you, love.'

She bent to scratch the top of the dog's head. 'Hey,
buddy. Hey there.' She straightened up. 'Nice dog,' she
said. 'Take it easy, both of you.'

'And you,' he said. 'God bless.'

She was a good, good person.

We stood there a moment longer.

'Can I ask you something?' I said.

'Ok,' she said, 'you can ask.'

'What advice would you give your twenty-seven-year-
old self?' I asked, cringing even as I heard myself asking.

Rachel arched an eyebrow. She looked faintly dis-
appointed and faintly amused, both at the same time.

'Twenty-seven, huh?' she said, and it was all I could do
to stop myself blurting out, Yes, today.

She sighed. Under the orange streetlights she looked

even older than I'd thought: she could be forty, I realised. I couldn't tell anything for certain any more.

'If something doesn't work out,' she said, 'a date – an encounter – it's not necessarily your fault. It's not necessarily anyone's fault.'

'Ok,' I said.

'I'd also say,' she said, 'don't rush to give away all of yourself, instantly, because someone has happened to express the slightest interest.'

She paused, and I waited for her to go on, but she didn't.

Black taxis were cruising past the boutique hotel just down the road, and Rachel put her arm out. 'I'm going to get you a cab,' she said. 'I want to make sure you get home safely.'

'I want to walk,' I said.

She sighed. 'Whereabouts exactly are you?'

'Weavers Fields.'

'Ok,' she said, 'come on.'

'You don't have to,' I said. 'Seriously. Honestly, I'm fine.'

'If something happened, I'd feel responsible,' she said. 'I'll walk with you. Only we might have to get some falafel or something on the way.'

'Sure,' I said. 'There's that place on Brick Lane, by the railway arches, if we go that way?'

There was a queue outside Damascu Bite. We leaned against the wall as we waited to place our orders, breathed in the apple shisha and listened to the Syrian radio station the owner always played.

39

'I want to say again,' said Rachel, 'I really, really don't want things to be awkward for you at work. Will you promise me it's going to be ok?'

'I don't even know your name,' I said. I laughed, but it might not have been entirely a laugh.

She looked at me. 'Are you taking the mickey?' she said.

'Your full name,' I said. 'Your real, whole name. I have you in my phone as *Rachel Work*.'

Now it was her turn to not-quite-laugh. 'Ok,' she said. 'Ok.'

For a moment, neither of us said anything. Through the serving hatch, the owner shaved his shawarma and flipped slices of halloumi on the griddle, rattled the handle of his deep-fryer and shouted out finished orders, all in a sort of dance. We were next-but-one.

'Falafel wrap with everything?' she said.

'Sounds good,' I said, and I realised as I said it that it did. I hadn't really been eating recently, besides the vegan (of course they were) salads I pretended to appreciate. 'But seriously, I'm paying for this. It's the least I can do.'

'Ok,' she said. 'Thank you.' Then she said: 'Eleanor Anastasia Rachel Cooke.'

'What?' I said.

'So now you know.'

'Eleanor,' I said, 'Ana*stasia*?'

'Eleanor Anastasia Rachel Cooke.'

'Why do you go by Rachel?'

'I always hated my name,' she said, and shrugged. 'It was so – showy. So extravagant. When I started secondary school I decided to become just Rachel.'

'But Eleanor's a beautiful name,' I said. 'And Anastasia! I mean, not that Rachel isn't, I just mean—'

She looked at me. That suddenly-familiar, wry, amused, crinkle-eyed expression.

'I'm sorry,' I say, and it's true, I am.

'Come on, you,' she says. 'You're drunk. Let's get you home.'

Words for Things

We were talking about Monica Lewinsky.

My friend had googled her, some late-night internet rabbit hole, and had realised that, when it all happened, she'd been just twenty-two.

Fuck, I said.

I know, right? Twenty-two.

Neither of us said anything more for a bit. We rocked our buggies absent-mindedly back and forth. Sometimes I rocked the buggy when the baby wasn't in it. Sometimes I rocked shopping trolleys.

We'd just come from our baby swimming class, thirty minutes of trailing wet bundles in thermoprene suits, who ranged from bemused indifference to howling impotence, around a hotel's basement pool, singing made-up extra verses to old nursery rhymes. *If you see a crocodile, don't forget to scream!*

We were standing outside the hotel's back entrance, preparing to push our buggies their separate ways. The babies were uncharacteristically silent, glazed and stupefied in the way I remembered being after swimming as a child, although they hadn't exactly done much of the work. It was spring, but cold. My friend tucked a stray hair under her yolk-yellow hat. Our babies, born within a month of each other, were just old enough now that our hair was starting to grow back: soft, stubborn wisps, and the relief of no more frantic hairballs choking the plughole.

Well, my friend said. I want to get home for his nap. So I should get going.

Twenty-two, I said. Do you remember what you thought at the time?

How stupid she was, I think.

Yeah, me too.

We'd been sixteen, seventeen, and certain it was Monica Lewinsky's fault. I remembered discussing it with school friends in the sixth-form common room. The stupid wee bitch, we'd called her. The silly wee slag. And the dress, like! The president had come to Belfast a couple of years earlier. He'd ousted the Power Rangers to turn on the Christmas lights; there'd been cheering crowds in Donegall Place, and fireworks. The Leader of the Free World. What did Monica Lewinsky think she was at? His daughter was more or less our age: frizzy hair and braces. We felt scundered for her, and disgusted.

I remember my mum saying how charismatic he was, I said.

That's one word for it.

Ha.

And do you know that The Dress was only from Gap? It was just this . . . shirt-dress thing. Bog-standard blue.

I had imagined some chi-chi cocktail dress. Marabou feathers, a plunging neckline.

Yeah, my friend said. She never got it cleaned to wear it again cause her friend said she looked fat in it.

We both had a fit of giggles and the babies regarded us with their disapproving stares.

I'll walk with you a bit, I said. I turned the buggy and we fell into step. We were both wearing trainers, hers trendier than mine. It had been a joke between us for years, my impractical footwear. I thought of how substantial my first hi-tops had felt, after years of flimsy ballet pumps, the cheap ones made out of cardboard and fake leather. When we'd discovered how well made men's brogues were we'd laughed and laughed.

Her bus was pulling in to the stop, and we ran for it.

Come back to mine, she suddenly said, for baby rice and Ella's.

But there was already a buggy on board, and the maximum allowed was two. We hugged a quick goodbye, chlorine and cold cheeks, and see-you-next-weeks.

It wasn't for the babies we did baby swimming, of course.

A minute or so later, my phone buzzed: a stream of emojis telling the story of two splashing whales and two fishes abruptly and tragically separated. Then another message, tactfully upgrading the whales to dolphins, with the crying-laughing face.

I didn't know when we'd started to communicate in emojis, but I was pretty sure it had coincided with parenthood. A way of acknowledging how forthright, earnest, certain we used to be about everything. Or maybe it was just sleep deprivation.

I sent the same face back, then searched for the bowl-of-rice and the strawberry and wrote: Enjoy your pre-digested feast.

She sent me the Edvard Munch face, and some x's.

There was no way I'd make it home before my baby fell asleep. But if I started walking now, I could sit in a cafe and google Monica Lewinsky for five minutes before he realised the buggy was no longer moving and woke to express his outrage.

As I walked, I thought of our early twenties. We'd spent them putting the world to rights over cocktails of Żubrówka and apple juice at bars that used to be handbag factories, or in bedsits over mugs of herbal tea, the same freewheeling conversation that continued for years, it seemed, lightly spanning the places we and our other friends variously sojourned, internships, relationships, the occasional Alpha course. Brussels, Paris, London, New York: big cities with bright lights, flatshares and failed love affairs and flea markets on Sundays. We'd thought we were living the dream, and if we were unhappy, well, it was our fault, our failure to live up to it all.

Once, at a bonfire party, we'd talked late into the night, long after the others had gone, moving our chairs now and then towards the warmth. At one point we'd looked down to realise the embers were smouldering around us. It had seemed, at the time, a metaphor for something.

I took my phone from my pocket and swiped it. Do you remember the bonfire? I texted, still walking.

Her message flashed back before I'd even suffixed some flames.

There'll soon be less distance, it said, between our babies and us-then, than us-then and us-now.

It took me a moment to get my head around it.

I sent back the smiling-crying face and the Edvard Munch.

On a whim, in the aisles of the Costcutter, I bundled the necessary packets and tins into my basket, and when I got home I made Fifteens.

They were called Fifteens because you needed fifteen of everything. Fifteen digestive biscuits, fifteen marshmallows, fifteen glacé cherries – the stickiest, most artificial, reddest sort. You bashed the digestives with a rolling pin, halved the cherries and marshmallows, mixed up the whole lot with a tin of condensed milk, then rolled it into a sausage and shook over desiccated coconut. You didn't even need to cook it, just chill it for a bit. It was a ridiculous recipe, and one that could only come from a place where grown men and women would, with a perfectly straight face, order a square of Lumpy Bumpy to have alongside their pot of tea. A place whose facade was allowed, or needed, to slip just that much, no more.

We had made Fifteens in primary school – everyone made them in primary school – and I still remembered the stout headmistress sliding her finger around the inside of the tin of Carnation condensed milk and shivering, rolling her eyes with pleasure.

She'd taught us penmanship, and stepped into the class-room unannounced to drill us on times tables. Her hair was tight with perfect curls and she walked with a rubber-tipped stick which she sometimes thumped on the floor. Once, in Supermac, at her wits' end with our bad be-haviour, my mum had threatened my sisters and me with the idea that our headmistress could be right around the corner. We'd turned into the next aisle, and there she was. I'd been in awe of her for years after that, as if, rather than the force of my mother's summons, the power to appear had been hers alone.

I hadn't thought of the headmistress for years. I tried to work out how old she might be. I realised that, by my friend's logic, I was nearer to her age then than she would be now. If she was still alive. She had retired when we left primary school. I tried searching for an online obituary, though I didn't know her first name, didn't know, in fact, if she'd taught and lived under entirely different surnames. No, I realised; that couldn't have been the case. Teachers back when she started out had to resign upon getting married. I googled some more. I came across a young Nell McCafferty, in the mid-seventies, leading a charge of thirty women into a pub. They ordered thirty brandies and one pint of Guinness. When the barman refused to pull a pint for a woman, they each drank a brandy then refused to pay, on the grounds that their order had not been fulfilled. I could still hear my headmistress's voice. I decided she would have approved entirely of the enterprise.

I closed the little window on my phone. It was time to wake the baby, still out for the count in the hallway, or he'd never sleep tonight. Before I woke him, I cut a corner off the roll of Fifteens. It was too sweet, of course: far too sweet. I thought once more of the headmistress and her theatrical pleasure. Then I ate two or three more slices.

The baby woke beaming, as if seeing my face was the most wondrous thing ever, and I ached with love for him. We spent the afternoon in bed, feeding, cuddling, practising tummy-time. I amused us both, or at least myself, by making up more alternative verses for songs. *Three little people in a flying saucer flew round the world one day, they looked left and right and they really liked the sight so they came for a holiday.* The baby was in a playful mood, gurgling and babbling, so I took a video of him squealing with pleasure as I kissed his toes and sent it to my family group. We'd communicated more, in the few months since the baby was born, than we ever had before, and it was almost entirely through the medium of him.

awwwwwwwwwww

my youngest sister said, almost immediately

sooooo cute

Words for Things

give him a kiss from his aunty

My youngest sister messaged like the Millennial she supposedly was and I definitely wasn't, despite the barely-four years between us: one line at a time, rarely any punctuation, and all lower-case. If she and her boyfriend were annoyed with each other, they would zap back and forth gales of messages one word at a time.

seriously

you

are

such

a

complete

and

utter

dickweed

sometimes

My middle sister, from whatever time zone she was in, sent hearts-for-eyes.

Mum is typing . . . my phone said.

Mum is typing . . .

There wouldn't be any response to the video from my dad. He caught up on all his messages once or twice a week, texting like the digital immigrant he was: long, single texts riddled with elisions and compressions (cu 18r), muscle memory from when you – or rather he – paid per message for all phones on the family account, and characters were limited.

Mum is typing . . .

Mum is typing . . .

I thought about my first-ever Nokia, and how miraculous it had seemed back then: the little envelope that showed a new message had come in; the string of flashing letters slowly scrolling across the small grey-green screen.

Mum is typing . . .

My mother, true to form, eventually sent a gif. She had recently discovered gifs and communicated almost exclusively, if often erroneously, through them. This one was a key moment from *Flashdance*. Despite having three daughters, I doubted she'd ever seen the film. On the spur of the moment, I rang her.

Hello? she said, sounding surprised.

Hi, I said. I just thought I'd ring.

Oh, lovely, she said. I'm in the Tesco's car park.

Oh, sorry.

No, no, it's nice to talk. Hang on.

There was a pause while she did whatever she did. My mum never phoned me, in case she disturbed me, she said, or woke up the baby. But I called her almost every other day now.

You saw the video? I said, when she came back.

Yes, did I not reply? she said. I thought I'd replied.

No, no, you did. Have you ever seen *Flashdance*?

What's *Flashdance*?

Never mind.

Well, my mum said brightly, so how are you?

Good, I said. He's very sweet, isn't he?

Oh, he really is. I remember you at that age, when you suddenly started crawling. Just suddenly, out of nowhere. It was Christmas Day. You couldn't even sit up properly, but there you were, hauling yourself across the floor to get to some shiny wrapping paper.

She laughed. Then she said:

You'll never be loved so much again.

Sorry? I said.

It goes so fast, she said. Then she said, brisk now, Well, I'm at the car, and it's starting to rain, and I've got to get the dinner on.

Mum? I said.

Sorry? she said. Hello?

No, nothing, I said.

Keep sending the photos and videos. We love seeing him.

I will, I said.

My mum, in the Tesco's car park. Starting the engine so

the heat would come on, then sitting there for a minute, before edging out of the parking space and joining the traffic on the slip road to the Sydenham bypass. The clouds over the Holywood hills would be thick and lowering in a waterlogged sky. The Stena Line ferry chugging in over the lough; the Irish Sea.

You'll never be loved so much again. It was no more than I'd been thinking myself, since my son had woken. But I felt the ache all over again, the inevitable and necessary complication of that love. Something my friend and I discussed almost every time we met: was it harder, these days, raising sons or daughters? And how were we not to fuck it up?

What do you think of, I said to my husband that evening, when you think of Monica Lewinsky?

It was Friday night so we were having a glass of wine while we looked at our phones.

My husband didn't miss a beat.

I did not, he said in a hick voice, while continuing to swipe at his screen, have sexual relations with that woman.

But he did, though.

My husband looked up at me.

Course he did. Did anyone ever doubt it?

Well – yeah. Or at least – they wanted to.

Plausible deniability.

The baby monitor squatting in between us crackled ominously. We waited to see if it was something or nothing. It was something.

I'll go, my husband said, even though he'd gone the time before.

Thank you, I said. If parenthood was seventy per cent trying to get a baby to sleep, twenty per cent trying to keep it awake, and ten per cent texting each other lists, then maybe this was true love.

While my husband was gone, I texted a new name to my friend: Anna Nicole Smith. We'd spent the afternoon sending names back and forth. Tonya Harding, Amy Winehouse, Shannen Doherty, Britney Spears. Because the thing was, it wasn't just Monica Lewinsky. It was all the other women too, who used to be sort-of laughing stocks, and who – you suddenly realised – turned out to be something else entirely. Once you started googling, it was hard to stop. Anna Nicole Smith's son, Daniel, I now newly knew, died suddenly in her room in hospital, while visiting her and her new baby, his half-sister. The toxicology report suggested he'd ingested some of her methadone prescription, along with other medication. At his funeral, she made them open the coffin and tried to climb inside: she begged them to bury her with him. He was twenty, and she was only thirty-eight. She died of an overdose herself a few months later.

Good one! my friend messaged back. A moment later, she texted: Jade Goody.

Jade Goody! I replied.

My friend sent the hand-painting-its-nails.

How could we not have known? I wanted to text, but I couldn't think of the right emoji to make it funny.

You knew, and didn't know. Sometimes it seemed that all of my life had been knowing and not-knowing. As if it was a technique rather than a state; a safety mode, a way of coping. There were words for things now that we hadn't even realised were things, because there were no words for them.

Do you remember, I said when my husband came back, Sinéad O'Connor ripping up the picture of the Pope?

Vaguely, he said. Not really.

Here, look, I said, and I found it on my phone.

She'd been performing on the American programme *Saturday Night Live*. In rehearsal, she'd held up a picture of orphaned children. *We have confidence in the victory of good over evil*. But when she did it live, the picture was of Pope John Paul II and she ripped it up, once, twice, three times, and scattered the pieces. *Fight the real enemy*, she said, looking straight at the camera. The clip ended with her taking off her headset and blowing out the church pillar candles on the table beside her.

We watched the twenty-nine seconds again, and then again. Every time, you felt something creeping up and down your spine.

Bloody hell, my husband said.

I can't believe you don't remember that, I said. Maybe it wasn't such a big deal in England.

I took my phone back and leaned against his shoulder.

We would have been eleven at the time, I said.

I remembered the shockwaves. One cardinal, in an interview on TV, said she was using voodoo or 'sympathetic magic' in an attempt to injure the Pope.

The cigar, my husband said, after a bit.

The what?

That's the other thing you think of. Or at least that you try not to.

A moment later, he said, I'm completely knackered. Shall we just go to bed?

It was nine thirty-five, which was at least five minutes past our bedtime. We'd been going to try to watch something.

Yeah, I said.

He set off the dishwasher while I plugged in the monitor to recharge.

There are times in my life, I said. It was a phrase that had recently entered our private lexicon, a shorthand of sorts.

I know, he said. It's nine thirty-seven now. Come on.

I couldn't sleep. It was too cruel, the nights this happened. Your exhausted body, flush with adrenalin, primed to jump at every cough and whimper, eventually refused to settle at all. I googled Monica Lewinsky again, and found the photo of the dress. It was on a cached eBay link, where someone was offering it, *not the actual dress itself lol*, for sale for a hundred dollars. Wouldn't some other museum want it? someone had asked in the questions. Like I think the Smithsonian has the original?

I looked at the dress, at pictures of Monica now, at pictures of Monica then. You didn't even need to type *Lewinsky*, the internet knew you wanted her. I found a fuzzy picture that someone had scanned in from a college yearbook.

I thought – of course, again – of myself back then. Of myself at twenty-four, twenty-two, nineteen.

We had done the Starr Report in my first week in college. It might, in fact, have been my first-ever lecture. The lecture theatre was packed to the rafters with not just freshers, but second- and even third-year students. The young lecturer was something of a celebrity on campus: I had picked that much up already, along with the slang for the dining hall and the porters' lodge and the woman who, to my shame, made my bed and emptied my wastepaper basket every day. They were all words that I couldn't bring myself yet to use, out of conviction they'd sound ridiculous coming in my accent, coming from my mouth.

The lecture was on prac. crit., 'practical criticism', the newest of the skills – or concepts – I had to master. How to close-read and analyse a text. I tried not to think of our teacher at GCSE, fresh out of teacher training and earnest, pressing us to explain why Wilfred Owen had selected a particular word. My friends and I sniggering, passing notes.

Because it rhymes? I'd said when she finally called on me, just sarcastically enough that my friends would definitely know it and she might not.

It's utter shite, all of it, the girl beside me had whispered. Sure he's there in the trenches, being shelled to fuck. He wants to get his poem on the page, he doesn't care what word he uses and why.

The lecturer, who was slim and angular, allegedly quick-tempered and also reputedly brilliant, stalked up to the lectern and immediately began reading aloud, while we fumbled for a copy of the handout being passed along the rows.

At one point, Ms. Lewinsky and the President talked alone in the Chief of Staff's office. In the course of flirting with him, she raised her jacket in the back and showed him the straps of her thong underwear, which extended above her pants.

He was reading from the Starr Report. He looked up, made a joke about the American versus the British word for undergarments and paused for laughter. Everyone, myself included, obliged. Carry on, he said suddenly, pointing at a blushing boy with steel-rimmed glasses near the front.

Ms. Lewinsky testified, the boy recited, '*I believe he took a phone call . . . and so we moved from the hallway into the back office . . . . He put his hand down my pants and stimulated me manually in the genital area.'*

Straight out of the Haynes Manual on Sexual Intercourse, he said, and we all laughed again, though I didn't know what the Haynes Manual was.

Let's hear that passage again, he said, and picked on someone else.

I believe he took a phone call . . . and so we moved from the hallway into the back office . . . . He put his hand down my pants and stimulated me manually in the genital area.

I'm still not getting it, he said. Again.

In the third or second row, I was desperate not to catch his attention. If he called on me to read aloud, or give an opinion, I'd freeze, I knew I would, and make a mockery of myself.

After the fourth time, he took pity on us, or maybe just got bored.

The *ellipses*, he said. Why am I not hearing the ellipses? The ellipses are the most important part of it.

He read aloud himself, then, in a falsetto voice.

I believe he took a phone call – dot, dot, dot – *and so we moved from the hallway to the back office* – dot, dot, dot, DOT. Poor prim, flustered, trying-to-be-dignified Monica, he said. I mean, look at those ellipses AGAIN – dot, dot, dot – dot, dot, dot, *dot*. Think about what they're saying, or trying not to.

While I tried to make myself invisible, while the president continued talking on the phone, while the lecturer strutted and joked, she dropped to her knees and performed ('performed', the lecturer said, how much of all this is a performance, and for whom?), she *performed* oral sex.

*He finished his call, and, a moment later, told Ms. Lewinsky to
stop. In her recollection: 'I told him that I wanted* dot, dot, dot
to complete that. And he said dot, dot, dot *that he needed to
wait until he trusted me more. And then I think he made a
joke* dot, dot, dot *that he hadn't had that in a long time.'*

Randy Bill hasn't come to completion, the lecturer said,
but like him we're done with Monica for now, although
she may yet come back to haunt us.

And we laughed and laughed: at Monica, with relief, at
the trope (a new word on me) of the dissatisfied husband,
and moved on to Wordsworth.

At the end of the hour, everyone, myself included, gave
a round of applause. It had been inconceivable to me that
you could put a verbatim account of giving a blow job
alongside the poems of Wordsworth, and read them with
equal attention and care.

I still remembered it, after all these years. Dot, dot, dot.
Dot, dot, dot, *dot*. What was said, and wasn't, and why.

He was meant to be very charismatic, my mum had said.

That's one word for it (my friend).

The beginning of the Starr Report, which I found now
on my phone: *When she introduced herself to him, he said he
already knew who she was.*

At least we —

I began to text my friend, my phone jumping to antici-
pate each word. It was 2 a.m., but her baby was teething

too, and even at this time of night, or morning, the little ticks often went instantly blue to show she'd read it.

At least we—

Then I stopped. I held my phone in my hand for a while, and concentrated on breathing, until I could feel my lungs release and fill, then deleted the characters, one by one.

Jars of Clay

THEY SPLIT UP AT CHECK-IN to give them all the chance of witnessing to their travelling companions. You never know, says Pastor Rick: it seems this going home to vote is really a thing, and you might just change someone's mind.

Her seat is by the window and the aisle seat is taken by a middle-aged woman with purple hair and thick-framed glasses. The seat between them is empty, which makes the woman her only chance. She waits until the plane is safely in the air (suppose I had wings, like the dawning day, and flew across the ocean; even then Your powerful arm would guide and protect me) before taking a breath and turning to the woman.

Hi there, she says. She can see the side of Steve's head through the gap in the seats in front and wonders if he can hear her. She clears her throat.

I was just wondering if you might have a minute to talk about your views on the right to life of the pre-born child.

The woman looks at her. Are you asking for yourself? she says.

It takes a moment for it to sink in that the woman means
her.

Oh my goodness, no! she says, and is glad Steve isn't listening after all. I'm part of a Youth Ministry, she says rapidly,
and we're travelling to Ireland to help convince people to
make the right choice next week.

Ok, the woman says. For a moment, she seems about
to say something else. But then she smiles and says, Honey,
I am with you one hundred per cent, puts her earbuds in,
and closes her eyes. When the drinks trolley comes
around, the woman opens her eyes to order two miniature bottles of red wine, which she opens at once and
pours into the same cup, almost to the brim. She thinks
about double-checking that the woman has accepted
Jesus Christ into her heart as her personal saviour, but by
the time she works up the courage to start a new conversation, the wine is finished and the earbuds are back in
place.

Wake me up for snacks, the woman says, putting on an
eye mask, but on no account let anyone disturb me for
anything else, and she just says, Oh, ok.

Evenings in Pastor Warren's house, practising.

What about in the case of rape or incest?

That was the big one and Steve's eyes were steady as he
said it, locked on Rebekah's. For a moment, Rebekah
didn't speak, and nobody breathed. Then she exhaled.

Both of those, she said, are terrible, terrible things. But

does an innocent child deserve the death penalty because of the crimes of her father?

The two of them looked at each other. Steve had been close enough that he could reach out and touch Rebekah's face with his hand. For a moment, he looked about to do it: to touch the faint sheen of sweat over her freckles, or tuck the loose strand of hair back behind her ear. His right hand formed a fist: clenched then unclenched. His earring glinting as it caught the light.

Does a woman deserve, he said, to be forced to carry her rapist's baby?

The circumstances of conception may be far from ideal. But adding murder to the equation will not make it better. Two wrongs do not make a right.

You talk about rights, he said. What about women's rights?

We totally support women's rights, Rebekah said, still holding his gaze. The only thing we don't support is society-sanctioned slaughter of the innocents.

Oh, come on, he said. It's just a bundle of cells.

The miracle of two tiny cells joining, and immediately the unique and complete genetic profile is already there, the blood type determined, the eye colour, hair colour, the set of fingerprints nobody else will ever have. Technology has shown us, she said, that as little as twenty-one days after conception a heartbeat is detectable. Do we ignore this because it doesn't suit our purposes?

Ok, he said, about to parry back again, but this time she went on.

We need to remember that this is not about us. It's about

those that are relying on us to – literally – save their lives. Please, on behalf of those whose voices we cannot hear, look into your heart of hearts and do the right thing.

They must have been able to feel each other's breath, the heat of each other's bodies.

Ok, Steve said, and raised his hands, palms outward. Ok, you got me. Ok.

They had looked at each other for a moment longer, then a slow blush had spread across Rebekah's cheeks. She had looked away.

Across the aisle, Rebekah is watching a movie. She can't quite see what Steve is doing, can't see Pastor Rick and Jen at all. She leans her head against the cool wall of the cabin and looks out of the window. There is nothing to see: Ireland is five hours ahead and they have already hurtled into night-time. She has her study Bible with her, of course. She should read it, or pray. She should rehearse potential arguments in her head.

Is it ok to sanction sex-slavery or pedophilia, because 'people will do it anyway'?

Should we stop teaching the times tables in school, because the Christian Church agrees with math?

Wrong is wrong, even if everyone's wrong. Right is right, even if nobody else is right.

Instead, she thinks of the dermatologist's waiting room. You had to take a pregnancy test before he'd prescribe you Accutane, and once a month while you were on it. She came out of the consulting room and announced to her mom, Well, I'm definitely not pregnant again! She said it too loud, and a couple of people glanced at her as if she might be. The shame of it: she'd never even kissed a boy, only once held hands with Noah Dean. The shame of the green blister pack of Microgynon contraceptive pills in her washbag.

Isotretinoin had severe teratogenic effects, the leaflet that came with the Accutane box said. If exposed in the first trimester, a foetus had a 20–35% chance of serious craniofacial, cardiovascular, thymic and central nervous system malformations. A further 30% of infants with no gross malformations would have moderate to severe mental retardation, and up to 60% would have impaired neuropsychological function. They used to play a game when they were younger, goading each other with worse and worse scenarios. All of them, always, were adamant they'd have the baby. But she really would. She would have it and she would love it, whatever it looked like, however deformed it was. She would love it and nothing, nothing on earth, could change the fact that it would be hers, her baby.

The women at church, in various stages of pregnancy. Sweet and clean like dough, placid hands on their bellies, a faraway look on their faces. Their soft faces, shiny hair. Their air of knowing something none of the rest of us do.

Grace, she would call it if it was a girl, and something like Theodore for a boy.

She closes her eyes. Pastor Warren prayed over each of
them individually before they set off. His strong, warm
hands on her head: if she concentrates, she can still feel
the pulse of energy from them. Lord, since it is through
Your mercy this child of Yours has this mission, let her
not lose heart. Be she hard pressed on every side, let her
not be crushed. Persecuted, but not abandoned; struck
down, but not destroyed. Let her carry in her body the
death of Jesus, so that through her body the life of Jesus
may also be revealed. Amen.

They had ended by singing one of her favourite hymns,
'There Is a Green Hill', which Pastor Rick said was appropriate, as they were going to the Emerald Isle.

Steve had carried on playing the guitar after the final
verse, picking out sweet, intricate, mournful chords. The
familiar feeling rushes through her again; a yearning so bad
it aches.

In the youth hostel they unroll the banners and posters
they made back home, smooth the worst of the creases
away and tape them to bamboo poles. The biggest one is
six feet long, bright-blue letters on a background they've
painted with yellow stars. BEFORE I FORMED YOU IN
THE WOMB I KNEW YOU, it says, and underneath
they've squeezed in Jer. 1:5, for people who might not immediately know the reference. The call of Jeremiah is one
of Pastor Warren's favourite stories. 'Alas, Lord God,'
Jeremiah says, 'I do not know how to speak, for I am only

a child.' But the Lord tells him: 'Do not say, "I am only a child."' For to everyone I send you, you must go, and all that I command you, you must speak.' Then He reaches out His hand, touches Jeremiah's mouth, and says to him: 'Behold, I have put My words into your mouth.'

Pastor Rick leads prayers and tells them to try to get some rest ahead of tomorrow. He and Jen hug and say goodnight; even though they're married, and could have asked for a private room, they're staying in the dorms like the others. She looks away, to give them some privacy. Rebekah makes a heart shape with her fingers. They are all praying that Pastor Rick and Jen, who have been married almost two years now, be blessed, as soon as possible, with the children they desire.

It isn't going to happen if you sleep in separate rooms, a mean, snide part of her thinks. She pushes the treacherous thought away.

The morning comes too soon, just minutes, it seems, after she and Rebekah and Jen have managed to fall asleep. In the dining room, her stomach turns at the thought of the eggs, sitting pale and flabby in circles of oil on the hotplate, but Pastor Rick insists they tank up in the face of the day to come. She forces a few mouthfuls down, mainly toast, and sips a cup of scorched coffee. Probably this is what people mean by morning sickness, she thinks. The Pill, after all, works by tricking your body into thinking it's pregnant. The thought makes her skin tighten and her insides loosen in a peculiar way. Lord, let me carry in my body the death of Jesus; let me renounce my secret and shameful ways.

They set up between the university and the main shopping street, near the statue of Molly Malone. Pastor Rick takes a selfie of all of them beside Molly Malone for the news-letter, then deletes it because it looks indecent: his head and grinning mouth inadvertently tilted towards the statue's heaving bosoms. She's glad he's deleted it. Her mom always sang them the song when they were little and she's certain that Molly was a little girl in it, not a buxom woman. Besides, in the photo she's clearly taller than Steve. They take another selfie instead, against the railings with their Jeremiah banner visible, and then they fist-bump and get ready to roll.

It's not what she thought it would be. Some pro-life cam-paigners stop to introduce themselves, and they all hug and swap some pamphlets, but hardly anyone else stops to talk: or if they do, they have made their minds up already, and just want a fight.

Yous are wrong, one passer-by yells at them. Wrong, wrong, wrong, wrong, wrong.

I'll pray for you, Pastor Rick says, and when the woman says, Oh, believe you me, you can keep your prayers, he just repeats: I will pray for you, ma'am.

We all will, adds Jen. You have a nice day.

Oh, I will, the woman says, eyeballing each of them in turn.

You do that, Jen says, super-sweetly. Rebekah giggles.

She just looks away and scuffs her ballet pump against the sidewalk.

Hey, Steve says. Hey. Don't let them get to you. Right is right even if nobody else is right, right?

She turns to him. It's the first thing he's said directly to her all trip. He grins and fiddles with his earring. She hopes her make-up, done in the harsh light of the hostel bathroom, doesn't look too orange.

Yeah, she says. Right is right, and she tries to think of something witty to say. But he's already turned away.

They work out a system, of sorts. Those who bring up septic miscarriage or the denial of cancer treatment in pregnancy go to Jen, who did a year's pre-med. People who quote the Bible – often maliciously, choosing deliberately contradictory passages from Leviticus or Proverbs – go to Pastor Rick. She, Steve and Rebekah take turns holding the banner, which they are not allowed to attach to city council property despite the theoretical freedom of speech in Ireland, and try to focus on the young people.

But the only young people who approach them are a group of teenagers who, after several minutes of watching and sniggering, come up and say, Why do Americans, like, use their entire faces when they say the word 'Ireland'?

That's not very nice, Steve says, and one of them says,

Yeah, well, neither is your unwanted involvement in our constitutional issue.

My family actually comes from Ireland, Steve says, and for some reason they find this hilarious.

Her family is from Ireland too: her great-great-great – she gets confused with the greats – great-something grandmother sailed to Staten Island from Cobh, which she knows is pronounced 'Cove', sometime in the 1800s. She's been wondering if there'll be time to go there at some point on this trip; it looks to be only a couple hours' drive.

A man stops to say, Fair play to yous all. He insists on shaking each of their hands with his liver-spotted one. Fair play to you. Fair play. It's the good Lord's work you're doing. She feels the glow spread through her again. They could set off at dawn, and if they made good time, be back by mid-morning. Play music on the way. You have to be twenty-one to hire a car, so it would have to be Steve who did it, but she has the money her mom gave her, for emergencies. She hasn't dared to mention it yet. Rebekah's family are from Sweden, originally, hence her blonde hair. So probably Cobh will mean nothing to her.

She has just handed the pole to Rebekah for a stint when the woman approaches.

Excuse me, the woman says. Excuse me.

The woman is talking to her.

Hi there, how are you doing today? she says, and smiles

her widest and most welcoming smile. But before she can offer a pamphlet, the woman says, I had a diagnosis of FFA at twenty-one weeks. Do you know what FFA stands for? She takes a breath. Ok. She knows the answer to this one. I'm sorry for your loss, she says, but the woman is already talking, talking over her.

It stands for Fatal Foetal Abnormality, the woman says. I had a diagnosis of Fatal Foetal Abnormality last year at twenty-one weeks. It took us two years to get pregnant. Two whole years. And then they did the scan and they told us. There was nothing they or anyone else could do. He wouldn't live more than five minutes outside the womb.

The woman's voice is low and calm. She has crinkle lines around her eyes that make her look as if she'd easily laugh, in other circumstances.

I'm sorry for your loss, she says again. It might bring you some comfort to think of the words of David in Psalm 139. Your eyes saw my unformed body. All my days were written in Your book and ordained for me before one of them came to be.

He had no days, the woman says. If he had survived the birth, he would have asphyxiated in minutes, in great suffering and pain.

But he chose you, she says.

Who chose me?

God chose you. And your baby – he chose you too, to be his mother, no matter how brief the time.

How can it be both?

Excuse me?

71

If God chose me, how could it also be the baby's choice?

She glances over at the others. Pastor Rick is earnestly talking with someone else, Jen is frowning over her cell phone, and Rebekah is laughing with Steve; nobody catches her eye.

God has a plan for us, she says, and it's up to us whether or not we fulfil it.

My love, the woman says after a moment, I can see you mean well, but you know nothing, nothing of life.

She says it tenderly, with great care. They have been shouted and jeered at all day – even spat upon. No one has talked with such kindness, as if they too are concerned about you, as if they too can see through your hoodie and jeans and zits to your immortal shining soul.

She focuses on the woman's lips, and tries to remember the answer because the right words, now, will win the woman over, and the wrong ones will lose her forever. Out of nowhere, she wonders what it would be like to kiss the woman. The shock of the thought repulses her and she feels her neck and cheeks flush with heat.

Hi there. Rebekah sidles over. Is there something we can help you with today?

She feels the woman's eyes still on her for a second. But then the woman steps back.

No, thank you, she says to Rebekah, and smiles a bright smile. I've got to be going.

Can I interest you in one of our pamphlets? Rebekah calls, but the woman's already walking away.

Look back. Look back.

Jars of Clay

But of course she doesn't look back.

All good? Pastor Rick says.

It was a Fatal Foetal Abnormality, she says. They were told the baby wouldn't survive outside the womb.

Alrighty, Pastor Rick says. So did we talk about the joy of holding your own baby, however briefly that is? Did we mention donating any functioning organs to others who so desperately need them?

Yeah, no, she says. I actually didn't manage to get that far.

Pastor Rick frowns. He has a GoPro camera strapped to his chest, in case of misunderstanding or assault, and to edit into a film of the trip for folks back home.

GoPro off, he says. When the little light goes out, he says, Hey, go get a soda.

I'm fine, she starts to say, but he holds up a finger.

There's a shopping mall right across the way. Take a breather, grab a soda and a bite to eat. He produces a note from his pocket, like a magic trick. On me.

She takes it. Thank you, she says. Okey-dokey.

You're doing great, kiddo, he adds. Jet lag can be a doozy.

In the mall, she buys a Pepsi Max and some fries, and sits at a table stirring the ice. The two old ladies at the table next to her are eating burgers with polite, meticulous bites and discussing the vote. She should jump in, introduce herself, ask them how they're planning on voting. Every encounter, every opportunity, counts. She drinks her soda too fast instead and her sinuses ache.

Summer afternoons after Bible camp, pooling their quarters and nickels and debating which flavour slushie to go for. The boy with the brown hair at the slushie stand they all had a crush on. Daring each other to ask him if the bubblegum had made your tongue go blue. How freaked out they'd have been if he'd ever responded, in any way. Knowing the pure, sacred temple of your body was saved for your husband and the children you'd make within. How cool would it be, Steve said, if your first-ever kiss was at the altar, beneath the eyes of God. Which, actually, didn't make sense considering God saw everything anyway.

She stands up. She hasn't touched the fries but she should be getting back.

The opposite side have a stall set up outside the shopping mall, with sweatshirts and Ts, that she had to scurry past on the way in. A girl with pink hair is hollering at passers-by now that they have just one t-shirt remaining. It's the white one, with a red heart across the chest. She wonders, for a split second, about buying it from them with the rest of Pastor Rick's money. It was the last one on the stall, she'd say. I bought it to stop someone wearing it flagrantly. But of course they'd say that the money, the money given in good faith by good people, would still be going directly to fund the slaughter of tiny innocents, whatever your intentions, however good the joke.

She is suddenly furious with the woman. None of the others have taken a break. It was Pastor Rick's idea, and he said it kindly, and made sure the camera was off, but nevertheless it will have been noted. By their fruits you shall know them. There are thousands of poor, hopeless, helpless unborn babies depending on her. I'm sorry for your loss, is what she should have said. But to put it bluntly, one tragic personal tale doesn't mean that anyone should be able to kill a baby whenever they like.

Maybe it's the jet lag. Maybe it's the Pill. But it will all make sense again, she knows it will, the way it did back home, in the youth group, with Pastor Warren telling them how right and blessed they are, how there is only one truth, and how we too must be burning, shining lights; this treasure in jars of clay.

Night Waking

OUT OF NOWHERE you are suddenly awake, heart pounding.

Nothing. The baby is next to you in the bed, asleep. In the orange glow of the salt lamp, the room's shadows are still.

There is no noise from your son's room.

The baby whimpers. Sometimes you wake a second before her, as if your body knows. That's what the baby blogs say, the ones that say co-sleeping is fine. A mother's instincts will keep you both safe. Though maybe it's you that wakes her. The rustling of the duvet as you turn, the agitation of a dream. You lie completely motionless, waiting to see which way she'll go.

And that's when you hear it again.

It's the creak of a footstep in the wooden hallway, the sound of a footstep that's trying not to creak.

No.

You wait.

You know the ley lines of the flat, the trusted, navigable paths. The faulty joists in the timber flooring, guaranteed

Night Waking

to wake a sleeping baby, even when that baby will sleep through the full blare of police sirens on the road outside.

Again, nothing – although now the nothing is charged.

It's summer, so the heating's off; it can't be the pipes or radiators clicking to life. It's summer, so the balcony door is open, to let air into your airless flat. You're on the third floor and the glass box of a balcony doesn't adjoin those of the neighbours, so it's always seemed safe enough.

Your breathing sounds noisy. Your heart too, leaping like a trapped thing in your chest.

The baby snuffles and rustles and turns onto her tummy. Was that another footstep?

You listen with your fingertips, with every hair of your head.

You locked the door last night, you're sure of it. Or rather, didn't fully lock it, as the Chubb lock has been sticking, but flicked the snib downwards to disable the Yale. It's always been your husband's task, like the bins and the recycling and the washing of pans, in the wordless division of domestic labour. But he's away for two nights, of which this is the first – a symposium in Berlin. You don't always bother doing the blinds, with the evenings so long. Has someone been watching? You know more than you mean to about the families opposite, the dioramas of their lives. Has someone who knows you, knows your husband, seen on his Facebook or Instagram that he's away?

You listen, you listen. Your whole body aches with listening.

There was the man who came to rehang the front door, when it sagged on its hinges and kept jamming in the frame. For weeks afterwards you had missed calls from an unknown number. When you finally texted the number and said *Who is this?* a message flashed back instantly, *An admirer*, followed by a smiley face, and then a second message, *Wud u like 2 go 4 a drink?*

I think you've got the wrong number, you texted.

I dont think so (another smiley face)

I'm sorry, but I don't know who you are.

Yes u do

You didn't reply, and showed the texts to your husband that night. Do you want me to text, he said, and say I'm your husband or something?

Oh what, like back off, this chattel's mine?

You both laughed, and it no longer seemed so sinister.

You were pregnant at the time, though not enough that it showed. You'd felt nauseous, blurry; the man's arrival had jolted you from a midday nap – that first trimester tiredness that leaches from your very bones. You'd been blank at the door, almost rude, then overcompensated by faking brightness, offering tea, coffee, your stash of ginger biscuits. When he'd said, What I'd really like is a nice cold beer, you'd laughed and said, Sounds good.

You thought it must be him, though you couldn't be sure enough to contact the company. Besides, it wasn't as if he'd changed the locks, only the hinges, and no more messages came.

Night Waking

There hasn't been another noise for a while now: long enough that you allow yourself to think you must have imagined it after all. Or maybe you didn't imagine, but misheard and it came from your son's room: a flung arm hitting the bedstead, a book falling to the floor.

You should check on your son. He begged and begged, this evening, to sleep in your bed, the way he used to until the baby came. You almost said yes. You half-wanted it yourself, the warmth of his smooth body, the way he cuddles right into you as if skin is no boundary. But you knew you'd all sleep badly if you did: the baby would wake him and he'd wake the baby, she'd see him and think it was morning and time to play, so you stayed firm.

Your son has been frightened of burglars recently, and so you've been reading him the rhyming books of your own childhood from the library: the Robbers with names like Grabber Dan and Grandma Swag, thwarting and thwarted by Cops in an intricate, uneasy dance; the burglar who accidentally steals a baby and then goes straight, returning the things he's stolen.

You really should check on him, but somehow your body won't move. If there is someone in the flat – there isn't, you tell yourself, but if there is – then surely it's best you're all asleep, or seem that way? Let that person, or persons, take what they want and go swiftly. Your laptop is on the kitchen table, your bag's by the sofa. There's a ceramic apple of loose change on the bookshelf, mostly shrapnel. It shouldn't take long. It might be done already.

You try to remember whether the noises, if there were

noises, were moving towards the bedrooms or into the living room: getting closer or further away.

There's a drug problem in the area, groups of addicts on the streets like some dystopian film, abandoned needles and scorched crack pipes. You sometimes watch the drug deals from your balcony; teenage boys standing lookout on corners, their mini-messenger bags wedged with thick rolls of cash. The cars speeding the wrong way up the one-way street, the shuffle-run of the addicts once the drop-off's made. There have been leaflets from the police about muggings in the street, about home security. But there was stealth, not urgency, in the movements you heard.

Would-be rapists who creep into houses late at night and lie in wait for their victims, listen to them breathe. Abductors who take children to order: a little boy, blond-haired, no older than three.

Stop it. Now. Get up and check, the way you make your son do. No burglars in the wardrobe, no monsters under the bed.

You sit up.

The French teacher who told you when walking at night to hold your house keys in your fist and poke a key through your first and second fingers, a makeshift weapon. A novel where someone thwarts attempted abduction by piercing her captor's eye with a hairpin. You cast around the room. An architect's pencil, the sort that pushes up refillable lead through a bright, sharp point? A paperclip?

Night Waking

A siren streams past on the road outside, shrill and discordant.

You quell the bubble of a sob.

Your phone is in the corridor. You read an article about the correlation between cell phone radiation and cancer, which led you down an internet rabbit hole to official public health guidance by the State of California on how to reduce exposure to radio-frequency energy. Ever since, you've insisted that phones aren't charged in the bedroom overnight; the plug socket in your cramped bedroom is right by the baby's cot. And what would you do, anyway, missed-call your husband until he woke, then text that there might be someone in the flat? Message your family group, your sister thousands of miles away in another time zone, and ask her to phone the police?

What, the operator would say, is the nature of your emergency?

I woke, in the night.

You ease the duvet off your legs and get out of bed. Once you have babies, they say, you'll never really sleep again, even after the babies finally do. Your feet on the floor like the herd of elephants you're always chastising your son about. If there's anyone in the flat, they'll have heard you now. Abandoning your plans to sidle along the wall, you go quickly into the corridor, grab your phone. You stand for a moment. Nothing. Into your son's room. He's sideways in bed, half hanging out. You lift him, tuck him back in, press your lips to his neck. He moans. The baby, as predicted, has started to cry. Back into your bedroom, and pick her up. She stops crying, starts to rootle, but you don't feed her yet, just put her down in the cot where she can't fall out. To the sound of her outrage, you go down the corridor the other way, past the front door and into the living room.

Nothing and everything looks amiss.

It was the Venetian blinds hanging over the open door, clicking against the doorframe in the breeze. It was a block, and then another, toppling from your son's precarious tower, constructed with Duplo and cereal boxes and his baby sister's bricks, which he insisted you leave out overnight.

You slide the balcony door closed, twist the handle up.

You check the front door, move the buggy up against it, just in case.

The baby's cry is now at boiling point. Your son wakes up and calls out for you too. Some tiny, shameful part of you is glad not to be awake alone.

You should go to them. Scoop up your son and bring him into your bed, feed the baby and then all lie down together, the way families must have for centuries, the way animals do.

The sirens again, outside. More of them now, and louder, shifting in pitch and frequency. There is something still tugging at the edges of your consciousness. A framed map in the hallway, askew on its picture hook. You right it, and think: Was the frame always cracked? For a moment, you feel gloved hands on your shoulder, hot breath down your neck. Why would the blinds rattle on an airless night, or a tower suddenly tumble?

Something is happening, somewhere, you tell yourself, but not here, not here, not now.

The Children

TRUMPINGTON STREET IS SCULPTURAL IN THE SUNSHINE: slashes and rhomboids of light and stark shade. Traffic is heavy and the taxi travels slowly, the driver giving me the tour. The Fitzwilliam, the Pitt Building, Peterhouse. We've already had the Backs, the Mathematical Bridge, designed by Isaac Newton and made, the taxi driver says, without a single nut or bolt. Students took it apart once to see how it worked and were unable to put it back together. I know this isn't true. Newton died a quarter of a century before the bridge was built, and it does have bolts, iron spikes driven in at angles obscured from sight. I walked over this bridge almost every day for the best – or worst – part of three years. But somehow the moment to say this passed, and so I smile and nod and let my mind drift.

I'm writing a story about Caroline Norton, who *changed the lot of mothers forever* with her battle to reform child custody law, or so the blurb on her biography says. I have the biography in a tote bag, though that's as much as I've read of it so far, along with a sheaf of her poems, newly joined now by a raft of photocopies about marriage and Victorian law and women's quests for equality. I've just come from Girton College, the first women's college in Cambridge; dusty sunlight in high-ceilinged, book-lined rooms, parquet-floored corridors and a lunch buffet (poached salmon, potatoes, mixed sweetcorn and peas) under the patient lights of a hotplate in the Fellows' Dining Room. A communal jug of tap water, tasting faintly of pewter. Polite tones in respectable surroundings; it all sounds eminently reasonable; Caroline Norton's letters to the Right Hons, her pamphlets, her famous essay condemning child labour; her bills presented to the House of Lords. I'll read the texts, write the piece.

The ghost of my former self, indulged all this June day long, weaving on a rusty bike to and from the Sidgwick Site and the UL with a backpack of books, sitting earnestly on threadbare sagging armchairs, is lost to a sudden battery of car horns from behind and an outburst from the driver, who's pulled up abruptly somewhere he shouldn't. We're here. My husband and children are waiting for me in the Botanic Garden. I pay him and sling the tote over my shoulder and go, all else forgotten.

The following day, I find a lump in my breast.

It's not unduly concerning at first. I'm breastfeeding; it's probably nothing; it will probably go. It doesn't go. A week passes, then another. It is larger now, and definitely there. I google: breast lumps when to be concerned. Google suggests, as Google always does, that it could be terminal and it could be nothing. I phone the GP surgery, who – uncharacteristically – say they can see me tomorrow, name a time. Ok, great, I say, not sure if I feel reassured or more worried.

The next morning, dodging the breakfast scramble, I grab the untouched tote. The surgery is busy and always running late: it will be a good chunk of reading time. In the waiting room, blocking out the TV giving diabetes advice on a loop, the crying pre-schoolers at the vaccination clinic, the elderly man with a hacking cough, the mother chastising her bored fighting sons in Bengali, I take out the biography. *Cut off from her children after an acrimonious split, she went about changing the law for wives and mothers.*

Right, I say to the portrait on the cover, a languorous oil painting in an off-the-shoulder dress, gold-and-ruby bracelet and elaborate lacquered hair, delicately holding a quill. Here we go.

I skim through Caroline's parents and her early years until – as she puts it – she accepts a proposal of marriage so that her life can begin.

There's a whole story in the titles of Caroline's songs, the first things she ever wrote. From before her marriage: 'Rosalie My Love, Awake!', 'Dry Up That Sparkling Tear', 'The Home Where My Childhood Played', 'Never Forget Me Love'. Afterwards: 'Oh Sad, Sad is the Heart', 'Why Should I Sing of Days Gone By?', 'Love Not'. The Honourable – or not so – George Chapple Norton mocks her letters and her ambitions, sets her writing things ablaze. He buys himself a cabriolet with her royalties – the word comes from the French, meaning *caper*, because of its light, bounding motion – a fancy and entirely unpractical vehicle. But when the doctor tells her to get some sea air to relieve the nausea of her second pregnancy, she is forced to share a bed with the landlady to save money. He slaps her face, he beats her. He seizes her by the nape of the neck and dashes her down on the floor. He kicks her in the side so hard that she can't sit down for days. He pulverises her face so badly the sight of it makes her sister vomit. He orders her from 'his' seat at the breakfast table and when she refuses he takes the boiling tea-kettle and presses it down on her hand. Then he sits in her place and calmly eats his breakfast. She leaves him. He begs her to take him back. She takes pity on him and, for the sake of their boys, gives him another chance. Within two days, he beats her so badly she loses her unborn child. He leaves her bleeding on the floor and goes to shoot grouse in Scotland, refusing to pay the doctor's bill, leaving her to beg her brother for money. For weeks afterwards, she sits looking at raindrops on the window: *I begin to think I must have lost my soul.*

My name is called. But the GP wants a second opinion and asks me to return to the waiting room until her colleague is free. There are no chairs now so I stand against the wall. A weeks-old baby wails in pain and my body responds with the swell and rush of milk. I text my husband, who's meant to be back at work by now, instructions on what to feed the baby for lunch. I fish the book from my tote bag again, then hesitate. A moment: what we used to call *a goose walking over my grave*. This isn't how it was supposed to go. A second opinion. I was expecting, Oh, it's just a milk duct, use hot compresses and a comb. I was even prepared for, Let's aspirate it now, a dab of local anaesthetic and it'll only take a minute. It's suddenly not what I want to read about any more, mothers, children, loss. I text my husband again. It's all fine here, he texts me back, with a row of x's. Of course it is. He's a brilliant father. We're equal partners. But still.

Don't be silly, I tell myself, and force my hands to stop trembling and open the book.

Her brother tells her to come to his house in Dorset for Easter, with the children, without George. Her husband forbids it. She doesn't know what to do. She decides to wait until he's at work, then sneak away. But he makes his move first. She returns home one morning to find the children, and their nanny, gone.

Frantic, she manages to bribe it out of a footman that they've been taken to a lodging house in Upper Berkeley Street, ahead of plans to spirit them up north. She rushes to the house and begs the servants there to let her see her children, just for an hour, just for five minutes, just to tell them she loves them. But their master's instructions are clear and his threats severe, and they refuse.

The Children

I could hear their little feet running over my head while I sat sobbing below, only the ceiling between us and I not able to get to them!
Her eldest is recovering from scarlet fever. She doesn't trust her husband with their second, whom he taunts and dislikes, and the youngest is still a baby. She is desperate. But there's nothing she can do. The children are George's property, his to do with or dispose of as he sees fit, until they reach their majority at twenty-one. He sends them to his sister in Scotland. He changes the youngest child's name. When the middle child needs to be 'corrected', he is stripped naked, tied to a bedpost and whipped with a riding crop. She sees them one day in London for a few, snatched minutes. They are nervous wrecks, the middle one *a perfect skeleton*. They do not understand why she has abandoned them. They beg her to stay. Her heart aches with the weight of all that is impossible to explain. The following day, a message from her husband: the boys will not be seeing her again.

The years pass.

The second GP frowns and says carefully that although it is probably nothing, it is certainly something, and she'll refer me to the Breast Clinic at Barts. She taps away at her computer. I'll get a phone call in a few days to arrange the appointment. Out in the street, I finish the last few pages of the chapter I'm on. George writes to 'my Carry' that the boys are so grown-up that she would not recognise them, if she passed them in the street. He offers to send her portraits he's commissioned. He says she can see them again if she comes back and submits herself to him. He forges letters from her, including one to the children saying their father wants them to die so he'll have fewer of them to keep. He says she can have them back if she engages a female companion of his choice. When she agrees, he immediately backtracks. He tells her she can see them at Christmas. He writes that they have embarked on the steamer SS *Dundee*. The day after they should have arrived, he tells her they have not come after all. He says they can join her on holiday. She rents a house by the sea, lights fires, airs the rooms. Ten days after they are supposed to be there, they still have not come. George says she can see them in London instead. She abandons the house and returns to London. He says he's changed his mind.

You have made, she writes to him, *an orphanage of our lives.*

I text my husband to tell him I'm on my way home. All ok, I ask, with you and the children? All fine, he texts back, Ok with you? and my fingers, fumbling, don't know what to say.

There is a famous house on Folgate Street in Spitalfields, about fifteen minutes' walk from me (or twenty if pushing a buggy one-handed and trailing a child on a scooter). It belonged to a man named Denis Severs, and he left it as a museum of sorts – part-museum, part-art installation – with the intention that, as you walk through the doors, you feel that you are stepping through the surface of a painting.

The Children

The house's ten rooms are ten 'spells', from the cellar and the *piano nobile* to the smoking room and the boudoir, transporting you back to the Huguenot silk-weavers who first lived there in the early eighteenth century, and on through the Victorian era, following the family's – and society's – fortunes. The porcelain, the portraits, the clink of the old brass clock: it feels as if the house's real inhabitants have just momentarily left the room that you've stepped into. Or so the website says. You cannot wear stiletto heels or heavily ridged soles on your visit; it goes without saying that you cannot bring a buggy, or a boisterous child. They have night-time openings, which are called Silent Nights, where you leave your phone at the door, and general admission on Sundays and Mondays. My husband leaves work at lunchtime to come and look after the children in a nearby park so I can see the house. But somehow I've misread the website. It's a Wednesday: the house is closed.

They were not like us, the historian at Girton College said. We often think of the Victorians as basically the same as us, a bit stricter, more sentimental, maybe, but they were not like us at all. Imagine that almost everything we believe, all that we take for granted, is overturned. That's how far we are from them, that distance and then some again.

They tell you to allow a whole half-day for the clinic. There are ultrasounds, mammograms, radiographers, registrars to see; pieces of pink and white paper to be taken to different reception desks on different floors, filed in different buff-coloured folders. I find a corner seat, then move when I realise it's by a rack of leaflets with titles such as: Cancer and Pregnancy, and Preparing a Child for Loss. The clinic is also the oncology centre and there are women here at every stage of treatment, from potential diagnoses to full-blown weekly chemo. There are women in wheelchairs, bloated with steroids. A woman my age takes the seat beside me and smiles brightly, about to start up conversation. She is wearing a hospital gown and has a cannula taped to the back of her left hand. I look away and make random marks in the margins of my sheaf of papers until I sense her resolve, or solidarity, waning.

In the various waiting rooms, I pore over Caroline's letters in digitised archives online, as she takes her personal loss and transmutes it into something greater than her, something heroic, enduring, revolutionary. Her handwriting elegant and legible even on the screen of a phone, the curve of her upper-case *I* and curlicue on upper-case *C*; the cups of *y*'s and *g*'s that are dropped when she's writing with haste.

She dreams her husband is dying, attended by two old women who berate her. She dreams an unborn baby has drowned: *I saw him float away and no one would attend to me because I was mad!* Since they were born, I've dreamed of losing my babies too. I dream that I've left my daughter in a Left Luggage unit and there are hundreds of dully gleaming lockers and I don't have a key. I get off a long-haul flight and my phone starts ringing: my husband, thousands of miles away, is asking where on earth I am and in the background the baby's crying, desperate for me, and it's too late to undo what I've done. I am dying, and I'm scared, and they tell me to keep calm and hold the hands that reach out for me, and I do, and feel myself pulled from my body. A moment's relief, then the agony of realising I will never hold my children again. I beg for one last chance and am let sink back into my body, sore and clumsy, and I take my boy into my lap and hold him tight, the smooth warm curve of his back, and know that this is all that matters, ever, ever, ever.

Caroline, without her boys – her Penny, her abandoned chicken Brin, her Too-too the little tadpole – stays awake all night long, night after night, staring into the dark, until visions of their large brown eyes swim up, *as when I looked up from my work and found them watching.*

She would be annoyed with them, then, for interrupting her; for breaking the spell. She writes – has always written – to survive. Her first novel paid for the birth of her son – the doctor's bills and the nurses. She accedes to her publisher's demand and writes a bijou almanac designed for the Christmas market: an inch and a half wide and sold with its own miniature eyeglass. She tries her hand at plays; she'll turn her pen to anything. She always has and has always had to, children or no.

She tests out guilt and refuses to feel guilty. Refuses shame too: there is too much fear of publishing about women, she writes. It is reckoned that they wish nothing better than to hide themselves away and say no more about it. *No longer!* she writes. She will tell her truth, and she will change the world.

When I can't concentrate on Caroline's letters any longer, I read Twitter instead, swiping, tapping, swiping. In the US, the children of asylum seekers are being taken from their parents at the border. There are photographs on social media of minibuses fitted with rows of baby-carriers for transporting infants to 'tender age' shelters. There is shaky hand-held footage and anonymous testimony. Children led away from their parents to be bathed, never to come back. Breastfeeding babies pulled from their mothers' arms. Sobbing toddlers clinging. A newsreader breaks down on live TV, unable to read the autocue. The US president rants on Twitter, self-righteous, or affecting outrage. I think of George Norton, suspicious, capricious, belligerent, ploddingly unintelligent, an ungovernable child. Foaming and stamping and rambling from one accusation to another, so that it was impossible to make out, wrote a clergyman attempting to mediate, what he wanted, or whom he meant to attack.

Laura Barrera, an attorney at the UNLV Immigration Clinic in Las Vegas, Nevada, tweeting from Paradise, NV.

@abogada_laura
5:55 PM – 28 Jun 2018
My 5-yr-old client can't tell me what country
she is from. We prepare her case by

drawing pictures with crayons of the gang
members that would wait outside her school.
Sometimes she wants to draw ice cream
cones and hearts instead. She is in
deportation proceedings alone.

I read and read the stories online, unable to look away. A
six-year-old who is blind, and her non-verbal four-year-
old brother, non-verbal in part because he's traumatised.
An attorney quoted on the BBC: 'Even a five-year-old
who wasn't traumatised can't always tell you their address
or what their parents look like or their last names. How do
you expect a child to do all that? This is not something that
the kids or their parents will ever get over.'

They do the scans; in a darkened room they do a biopsy.
The results will be back within seven to ten days; the receptionist makes an appointment for exactly two weeks' time
for me to come back and speak with the specialist. Back
home, I quiz my not-yet four-year-old son: What's your full
name? What's mine and Daddy's? What's our address? Half of
the time, he gets most of it almost right.

July. The UK prepares for the US presidential visit. On the
morning of 13 July, I watch over livestream as protestors
launch the huge inflatable baby, with its snarling lopsided
mouth and piss-in-the-snow-hole eyes, to float above the

Palace of Westminster. My son and I have made our placards, sellotaping pieces of A4 card to sticks of bamboo, and
we intend to join the protest march. But at the last minute,
the stupefying heat of the day, the thought of the swelter-
ing tube, my husband delayed on the other side of the city,
we – I – chicken out. My son is relieved: worried that the
man who steals children will try to take him. I will do this,
he says, and bares his teeth in a chimp-like snarl. I will do
that, and the bad man will run away. Then he buries himself
in my side. I want to stay with you for all the days and all
the nights.

Yes, I say. Yes.

Later, I look at the best placards on Twitter. Mary Poppins,
carrying her iconic umbrella, beside a slogan in rainbow
colours: SUPER CALLOUS FRAGILE RACIST SEXIST
NAZI POTUS. We will overcomb the hate. Orange is the
New Nazi. I'm missing Wimbledon for this, you Tangerine
WANKMAGGOT. Ours simply said BREASTFEEDING
BABIES BELONG WITH THEIR MAMAS, and even
more simply NO KIDS IN CAGES.

Caroline to Lord Melbourne: I wish I had never had
children – pain and agony for the first moments of their
life – dread and anxiety for their uncertain future – and
now all to be a blank.

In the evenings, after he's gone to bed, I arrange my son's
collection of dinosaurs to look like they're building a tower
with his sister's bricks, racing his double-decker bus and her
push-along trolley. I think of The Fairies who lived in my
doll's house and occasionally left letters, tiny writing in cards

no bigger than postage stamps, and packets of Parma violets.
But my sisters and I were older then: he will barely remember any of this. Do you remember before your sister was
born? I ask him, and he thinks about it and says, No! He
thinks some more and says, I hurt my knee in Croatia, which
is true, he did, a bad graze falling off a low wall, and the
shock of the blood made him howl for an hour.

In good moments, Caroline is convinced that there is
still hope. *Let them do all they can about the children*, she
writes, *I will undo in two hours what they have laboured to do
for ten years — I have a power beyond brute force to swing them
round again, back to their old moorings.* But mostly she feels
the lethargy of despair. *No future can ever wipe out the past,
nor renew it.* The children won't recognise her if she passes
them in the street, nor she them. The youngest is no longer
the fair, fat baby he used to be: those months, those years,
those precious days, are lost forever.

It is unbearable, the thought that a child will not remember its mother.

There is a psychoanalyst who says that at a certain moment
in pregnancy, if the mother-to-be is pregnant with a baby
girl, five generations fuse together. It comes at around
twenty weeks' gestation, when the unborn child, in her
tiny, seedling ovaries, makes the hundreds of tiny eggs
which will be her future children, or the possibility of
them. In that moment, the not-yet-child is already mother,
the not-yet-mother already grandmother, just as the

mother-to-be was once a possibility inside her own in-utero mother, carried by her one-day grandmother. I like the Escher's staircase of it, the sense of nestled Russian dolls. The potential grandchildren that I might never even see, joined in a vertiginous rush with the grandmother who only barely met me, the centuries collapsing.

But the psychoanalyst uses the image to explain how suffering is passed down the generations; how we become trapped in the behaviours of our parents and theirs, doomed to repeat destructive patterns, unless we find ways of breaking free. The iniquities, as the Bible solemnly tolls, visited unto the third and fourth generations. The loss of a mother may be played out in the souls of your children's grandchildren.

The lawyers at RAICES, Texas's largest immigration legal service non-profit, estimate that at least a quarter of the children, a number in the hundreds, will never, ever be reunited with their parents again.

I bought the psychoanalyst's book because someone quoted him on Twitter, saying that the US president was doing exactly the job he needed to, forcing into consciousness some of our collective unconscious issues. He told us not to look at him, but to look to ourselves. I didn't know quite what I made of this. The notion that we get the people we deserve, or require, seemed to let an individual off the hook; or, conversely, to imply that their achievement wasn't that great. I think of Caroline, and Abogada Laura. At night, the children tumble through my dreams. I wake in a tangled sweat. I can't even go to a fucking march.

The Children

In her cot beside me, the baby whimpers. I sit for hours, years, until my breathing calms.

She changes the law, single-handedly, but it's too late for her. The elder boys at ten and eight are beyond the law's reach; the youngest, so long as his father keeps him in Scotland, is beyond its jurisdiction too. Little William Norton dies of lockjaw – tetanus – one Monday in September, aged just nine, after falling from his horse and cutting his arm. The boys are alone and unsupervised at their uncle's house, the only servant the gamekeeper's wife, a hunched old woman who opens gates and locks doors. Willie makes his way to the nearest neighbour, Chapel Thorpe Hall, where he collapses and is put to bed. By the time Caroline's told that he's unwell, he has already died. She learns that he was conscious when he died, and begged for her, again and again.

The doctor tells Caroline that young Willie bore the painful spasms *with a degree of courage which he has rarely seen in so young a child*, as if this offers any consolation.

I am tired. I try to make my mind let go. This moment, and this, and this. Here, now; my baby's silky hair and milky smell. *A-duh*, she says, when she wakes in the night and wants milk. Online, a mother was alerted to breast cancer when her six-month-old started refusing to nurse from one side. Online, another, still nursing twins, died ten days after her diagnosis.

It is the night before the biopsy results. Somewhere, in windowless rooms, cells have been scraped and splayed on slides, dyed and magnified and studied, pronounced upon. I have finished the biography, and the letters, and now I read the poems until I know sections of them by heart.

> If the lulled heaving ocean could disclose
> All that has passed upon her golden sand,
> When the moon-lighted waves triumphant rose,
> And dashed their spray upon the echoing strand:
> If dews could tell how many tears have mixed
> With the bright gem-like drops that Nature weeps,
> If night could say how many eyes are fixed
> On her dark shadows, while creation sleeps!

The blue light of my phone gives me a headache. The day slides into dawn.

The hospital again, the staircase, the waiting room; a chair by the window, the rack of leaflets on the wall. The women with gypsy-style headscarves, or attached to IV drips; the occasional solitary man. Another young woman sitting stricken with her silent mother. My name is called. Everything you take for granted may yet be overturned.

And suddenly it's over. There is a name for it, and it's not exactly common, but it's benign. You can go, they say.

The Children

Come back six months after you finish breastfeeding, or at most a year from now, and we'll re-examine you to be on the safe side. They've changed the boxes on the form so the registrar can't find which one to tick, and then she does, and then it's done, the flimsy white paper to the ground-floor receptionist and out of there, into the merciless, beautiful, stultifying heat. I will make my life matter, I promise to the day. I will use my voice. I will fight for what is right. The promises well up in me. I will spend less time on social media. I will not take my husband for granted. I will never snap at my children again. My children. I will teach them that it's their job too to make a difference. I will try to be a good example. I will. I will.

Back in 1863, Caroline finishes a novel in which her heroine refuses to bow to shame. Beatrice Brooke is seduced and then abandoned by the rich, predatory Montagu Treherne; alone in Wales, her illegitimate baby boy dies. But Beatrice rebuilds her life: she sells her drawings and handmade lace, she moves back to London, becomes an artist's model. Against all odds and social conventions, *Lost and Saved* has a happy ending: Beatrice marries and has another child. This time, the reviews are split. Some call it a work of 'true genius', her best to date, but others are offended that a fallen women could be so redeemed. Caroline defends her heroine in the Letters pages of *The Times*, then starts work on her next and final novel, although of course she does not yet know it will be her last. Her middle son, *in a dreadful echo of my youth*, becomes increasingly violent, his wild and capricious moods taking dark turns. He flies into irrational rages and blames her for things that are not her fault, so that she is afraid to see him and hides in her room. He shoves her about and tells her to get out of his sight. He berates her in foul language. He hits her, and he hits his wife.

We go on. We endure, and go on. The old battles, the same battles, once again and in endlessly new configurations. On 24 July it is announced that the inflatable baby will travel to Sydney for the forthcoming US presidential visit there. On the same day RAICES tweets a plea to its followers to

Keep this in mind:

Children are still in cages. Parents still
don't know where their children are.
Some were coerced illegally into leaving
the country.

The media isn't writing as many stories
but the problem has not gone away.

Please, don't let up.

Lady Moon

THANK YOU, SHE SAYS. Tomorrow at two forty, the eighth floor, lift core nine. But before she's finished repeating it the phone has gone dead. She stands in the kitchenette. Underfoot, the squares of yellow linoleum tile are curling up from the floorboards. She edges one almost entirely loose with her toe then stamps it back down. Immediately, the woman below starts shouting. When they first moved in, she brought around home-made samosas and they accepted with exaggerated delight. But since then she's complained about them more than a dozen times: non-existent parties, imaginary fights. The landlord says he knows, it's happened before, but keep the noise down anyway. Now when she brings them food they thank her politely and tip it straight in the bin, even though that seems somehow unlucky. We've been looking for a reason to leave, is what they've been saying to each other. The pots and pans she clatters at midnight. The rotting piles of cardboard heaped along the fence. The sobbing arguments with invisible people.

The shouting fades to a grumble, then stops.

Tomorrow, two forty. The eighth floor, lift core nine.

There are two sorts of gin and a Japanese whisky on top of the fridge. A dusty bottle of Angostura bitters. An ancient cherry brandy, used once for cooking, and an unopened bottle of Baileys Irish Cream. They used to drink that in shots, when she was at school: Baileys and sambuca, a Slippery Nipple. A Screaming Orgasm had amaretto and Kahlúa in it too. It was the height of sophistication, at the Wolsey or the Boom Boom Room. She shudders. She has no idea where the bottle came from. She picks up the whisky, then puts it back. She could text Adjo: *Pick up a bottle of white wine on your way home?* But he'd know instantly, and she doesn't want to break it to him like that.

In the high, pale light of these lingering evenings, they have taken to sitting out on their roof terrace – not strictly a terrace at all, but the asphalt-covered roof of the building below, the elderly brother and sister's flat. There is a straggly jasmine in a pot that the previous tenants left behind, and she has bought some herbs ready-planted in a plastic tray: parsley, dill, rosemary and sage. The city exhales the sullen heat of the day. Music booms from a car pulled up below, the reek of weed, and they watch the aeroplanes forging their silvery paths in the almost imperceptibly darkening sky.

They have downloaded a flight-tracking app, at first a joke, but it's become oddly addictive, pointing a phone at a plane in the sky and waiting for the shiver and beep of information. The planes are normally mundane: from

Zurich or Frankfurt or Dublin or Aberdeen, almost all going to Heathrow, but occasionally they catch a Qantas flight, or the UPS from Louisville International to Cologne Bonn, or a private jet with all flight information obscured.

Adjo is late home from work and she is on the terrace when he finds her.

Hey, he says, clambering through the window and dropping down beside her, into the other of the rickety bentwood chairs they rescued from a skip.

Hey, she says, and she bends to pour the last few gulps of her water bottle into the plants, so that he doesn't have to see her face for a few moments longer.

Oh God, he says, and then again: Oh God.

They walk together to the Costcutter; a bottle of Chardonnay, overmarketed, overpriced.

We could carry on to Oddbins, he says, get something a bit nicer?

It's not a celebration, she says. It comes out more harshly than she intends.

Back home he cooks dinner, a little sheepishly, because he's still hungry, even if she's not, and she sits on a stool and watches him, sleeves rolled up around his biceps, the way he chops like a chef, left hand covering the blade, and she stops abruptly midway through her second glass of wine, just in case, and finally starts to cry.

That night she dreams of a house, a sprawling clapboard house beside the sea, white porch wrapped round three sides, and roses twining up the portico. She walks up the steps and onto the porch, down the side and around, in time to see a shining lady leading a little girl away. In the dream the lady turns to look at her, but the little girl does not; in the dream she doesn't even try to ask them to stay. She wakes up shaking and when he tries to comfort her, shrugs him viciously away.

They meet at lunch, an hour before the appointment, and wander aimlessly round the streets by the hospital, the low-rise estates with their shabby patches of communal grass, broken glass and dogshit and tangles of neglected roses, the occasional syringe. They perch on a low brick wall and Adjo reaches for her hand.

I did some googling, he says. It could be nothing. It could be – implantation.

The word is soft and apologetic in his mouth.

Yeah, she says. I just don't think so.

No, he says.

The GP didn't, either. I mean, that's why she—

Yeah, he says. Yeah.

On the phone, without even seeing me.

Yeah, he says again. After a bit, he says, We're on the same side here.

I know. I'm sorry. I know.

I love you, he says. We've got each other.

We've got each other, she repeats, and it's true, they have, and until a fortnight ago their life, their funny, poky little flat, their terrace in the evenings, seemed more than enough, more than they deserved.

Two forty, the eighth floor (lift core nine). The row of moulded chairs, bolted to the floor. The window out onto the city, the dozens of cranes, swinging over building sites in restless benediction. A memory: the P7 trip to Edinburgh, and the Camera Obscura where, with clever mirrors and a little piece of card, you could pick up a tiny beetling vehicle far below, watch it crawl over your card then fall abruptly off. People too: scoop them up like ants and pretend to blow them away and watch them scurry on, oblivious. She goes to tell Adjo this, then stops. There is no privacy here. Even when you try not to listen, you can't but overhear. *We went for a private scan and they couldn't find a heartbeat, they said to come straight in. Please, you have to see me now.* Two fifty, three o'clock. A couple emerge from the side room, ashen-faced. He can't work out how to open the main door, the right button to press, which way to push or pull, and she just stands there, slowly adjusting her hijab.

Five past, ten past, quarter past, half. Time isn't moving right. They've been here hours, a lifetime. Her name is finally called. The whole room looks at her as she stands up, then furtively tries not to look at all.

The brisk, matter-of-fact, not-unkind questions. The history, the dates. And any more bleeding?

A little.

Bright red?

More sort of . . . rusty.

Right then, let's have a look.

And then the intimate, impersonal violation of it.

You're doing great, the nurse says, and she replies automatically, as if it's a compliment, Thank you.

Adjo sits beside her, holding her hand, and his hand is too clammy, or hers is. The screen turned mostly away. The technician with her left hand tapping, bright acrylic fingernails. This is unbearable. Tears, wretched self-pity, swell up in her eyes. The technician adjusts the probe and the screen jumps, flickers.

Ok, she finally says.

Online, everyone seems fluent in this new language, a vocabulary of endometrial thickness and serial beta bloods, of hCG and IU/I and foetal poles. Their sentences rattle with acronyms: pg, mc, LH surge. Dpo, hpt, opk. Clomid, Metformin, doses, dates. Appeals for help: *PLEASE i need your success stories, please!*

As they left, the nurse had said: It could be earlier than you think, or a sign that things aren't viable. We'll wait a week, and take the bloods again.

What else did she say? *I have to say, the numbers don't look good.*

Online, a lady had low, slow-doubling numbers and is now twelve weeks pregnant with twins. Another had a routine ultrasound before a D&C and the technician found a heartbeat. The stories spiral unpunctuated into one another, occasionally with updates from the OP, original poster; or others begging to know how things turned out.

She scrutinises the numbers on her single-sheet report, rereads them to see if there's something she missed.

Gestational Sac: present.

Endometrial thickness: 25.0mm.

βhCG: 141 IU/I, requires serial hCG levels to be measured to establish a trend.

Google has translated each one of these things for her. Each one of those things, in Google, throws up despair, but also portals of hope.

She waits for the slow heat of the first blossoming clot. But two days pass, then three, and nothing. At the weekend they walk the length of the canal and come to a garden centre. COFFEES, TEAS, ICED DRINKS! a painted board announces, though inside the vintage Piaggio van is out of service. They wander up and down the little gravelled paths, the apple trees in sacks, the bay trees sheared into pom-poms. She buys, on impulse, something called a rhodanthemum, or Moroccan daisy 'Moondance', because the name reminds her of the Van Morrison song; a plant called nemesia that smells of vanilla; a hot-pink cosmos called 'Casanova Violet'. Back at the flat, lining them up on the lip of the terrace, she realises she needs proper pots, and compost to pot them in. A watering can. She should make a trellis for the stalk of jasmine too: get bamboo sticks and tie them into a lattice. Gardening string, or twine. They sit out all evening as usual. A Pakistan International Airlines flight, twelve minutes twelve seconds into its journey to Karachi. 26,075 feet, a speed of 424 knots. A Dublin flight, descending into London City, that's swung right out to Southend-on-Sea on its approach path, now at 1,841 feet and a ground speed of 88 knots and one minute of flight time remaining.

They can calculate it to the nearest foot, she says, gazing at his phone. And I mean, that's nothing: did you know they can work out to the nearest inch how far it is from any given point on earth to the moon? They both look up at the rising moon, pale in the sky.

To the nearest inch, she repeats.

There is a song she remembers her granny singing, a song her granny sang even after she'd lost the ability to have a conversation. *Lady moon, lady moon*, it went, *Sailing so high, drop down to Baby, from out yonder sky. Babykin, babykin, far down below, I hear you calling, I hear you calling, I hear you calling, But oh I cannot go.*

It wasn't planned. They're far from ready. They remind themselves of this. It was the last thing on their minds. They remind themselves again and again of this. They live in a flat carved hastily out of another, bigger flat; partition walls bisecting windows in odd places, a too-steep staircase with gaping open risers, a radiator behind the fridge-freezer, a terrace that's just a few metres of stapled, asphalt-sheeted roof. Adjo's only just finished the arduous seven years' study and she's still freelance; they can barely afford to juggle their masses of debt with the rent. They want to get engaged, and married. To travel: to India, maybe, or Thailand. Their tenancy agreement specifically states: *No babies*, right under the clause that says *No pets*. And yet. When they saw the pink line, faint at first, then darkening, the surprising thing they felt was joy. Terror, of course, and disbelief, but yes: joy. She felt her soul – her actual, indisputable soul, something she'd never really thought about before – swelling up until she felt too small to contain it all.

Monday, and Tuesday. Deep inside of her, infinitesimal numbers are conscientiously doubling, or falling, in their intricate, mysterious patterns. Tomorrow they'll know. On-line, people talk about ttc after mc. They used to say to wait, but now they say no need, in fact, *don't* wait, nature compensates and your body's more fertile. Within a month, within a couple of weeks, you could have your bfp again. She consumes the message boards in surges of self-disgust. It makes her feel squeamish, the hunger of these women. The way they pick through carcasses of intimate detail, for any shards of hope. The thought she might one day be one of them. Other things people say online. That even if a soul barely flickers on this astral plane, a week, a few days, it's still you it's chosen as its mother. That food should be mild, unctuous, and never stale or spicy. That damage to your root chakra can cause reproductive problems, as well as a more existential problem of not quite feeling, anywhere, at home. That the Law of Attraction aligns us to a reality that matches the way we feel, so that longing, much-wanting, must by its very nature lead you to an experience that lacks what you desire, or else how could you continue to long and feel more want? That everything happens for a reason, because what a cruel world it would be if we could only learn through pain, and how confusing the lessons if they only broke our hearts.

The evening before, she phones her mum, and her mum puts the phone on speaker so she can talk at the same time to her dad, and she can't find the words to tell any of it. How can she, until there's something to tell? She chatters instead about the painted houseboats on the canal, strung with fairy lights, the little garden centre, the pink-and-white daisies she bought, their names already forgotten, which amuses her dad, a keen gardener, as it's designed to. When her mum says, despite all this, You sound a wee bit flat, she just says, Oh, I've been a touch under the weather. Her parents have been married for thirty-two years, three children. At her age, her mum had her and was expecting her sister; they'd just bought a bigger, 'family' house. She knows they worry about her in London: not the knife crime, the drugs, the cost of things, but how hard it is to make room for yourself in the city, to put down any sort of roots. But London is Adjo's city; he'd never leave. And she belongs, now, to where he is. And even though barely a fortnight has passed, even though *it* – whatever it is, or isn't – is at best barely more than a sunflower seed, a grain of rice, they have already held each other close and talked long into the night about boy or girl, the colour of its hair, eyes, its skin.

Life, they tell each other now, will continue at the pace it was meant to: jobs, a nicer flat, their wedding. They've barely had a fortnight of these new sudden selves. This bright, implausible future.

All the People Were Mean and Bad

Two weeks after your cousin dies, you're on a night flight
back to London from Toronto. Your daughter, at twenty-
one months, too young for her own seat, but too old,
really, to be on your lap, is overtired and restless. Your
phone battery is dead. With no more cartoons, all you
have to entertain her while the plane taxis and waits, taxis
and waits, inching towards the runway and its take-off
slot, is the book your aunty gave her as you were leaving,
a book from your aunty's church. It's the story of Noah's
Ark, illustrated for pre-schoolers, the first in a series
self-funded and published by the church.

All the people, it says, *were mean and bad. Except for Noah.
Noah was good, and because he was good, God saved him.*

You hate this book.

Shall we look at the animals now? you say, but your
daughter says, No. She likes the animals, but she likes these
pages even better. Over a whole double-page spread, the
mean and bad people are doing mean and bad things: pulling each other's hair and laughing, aiming slingshots and
catapults at each other, gurning and scowling and spitting

and stamping their feet. You point at each of them in turn, naming their misdemeanours, and your daughter makes extravagant faces and laughs with delight.

Ok, let's look at the animals, you say firmly, and turn the page, but your daughter throws back her head and wails.

I'm sorry, you say to the man sitting next to you – the man who has the misfortune to be sitting next to you, for the remaining seven hours and thirty-six minutes of this flight; the only, admittedly small, consolation being it's a whole half-hour shorter than on the way there.

No problem, he says, and he starts to say, again, and unnecessarily, because he's already been too kind to you, lifting your bags up into the overhead locker and fetching beakers and bunnies and bribes of white chocolate buttons and finally the book from the stuffed chaotic tote at your feet, even getting up to ask the stewardess to rinse out a bottle for you in the galley, that he understands, has children himself, two sons – but the pitch of your daughter's cry is rising. You grimace an apology at him, and he smiles back then looks tactfully away, as if there's nothing to see at all.

Please, you say to your daughter, red-faced now and howling, Please, come on, Ma*til*da, shh, and you suppress the urge to shake her, or start howling yourself, and you turn back and take a deep breath and begin again: *All the people were mean and bad.*

There is one page in the book that you like: a page of blue, just blue, with a tiny Ark in the very top right-hand corner.

No words, nothing, just the sudden giddy perspective; the weight of all the fallen rain. It is, you think, the only truthful picture in the whole story.

Your daughter wriggles and cries for the whole ascent; but as the plane reaches cruising altitude, and the seat-belt sign pings off, and the in-flight cabin service begins, she finally falls asleep on your chest and you hold her, heavy and warm and limp and sprawling, and as her breathing shudders and lengthens you let your own eyes close. Seven hours and three minutes left. Just a little over three thousand miles. It seems more than time and distance you're traversing. It is a lifetime ago that you left London. And it will be one of the longest stretches you and your husband have ever been apart; by far the longest he's not seen Tilly.

You went with him on a couple of shoots after Tilly was born: one to Dublin, another to Cape Town. But it wasn't what either of you had thought it would be and it certainly wasn't a holiday, trying to placate a baby in unfamiliar surroundings, endless hours wandering alone or lying in a hotel room trying to sleep while half-waiting for him to come back. A driver, each time, at your disposal, but where to drive to, and when you got there, what to do? It was, in the end, far lonelier than being at home alone with Tilly would have been, and after those two trips, you didn't do it again.

You think of times apart early on, when you, or usually he, would be away, and of meeting each other again, at train stations or getting out of taxis, and how strange and shy you'd feel, wondering if he'd look different to how you remembered him, or smell wrong, and how sometimes, at first, you could barely look him in the eye. You've tried, for Tilly's sake, to talk every day: Cape Town is six hours ahead of Toronto, so you FaceTimed each night at her bedtime, his midnight, but he was inevitably still up, either drinking with the crew or trying to resolve more problems on an already fraught and overextended shoot.

You are trying not to think of it, this prolonged separation, as a separation; as a test.

Anything for your wife? the stewardess's voice says, and you open your eyes.

Oh, you say, we're not— just as he says, Oh, we're not— and he grins.

I think, he says, she needs a gin and tonic too? and you smile and say, Yes, thank you, that sounds good, and the stewardess scoops the ice and drops in lemon and opens the little green bottle and flips the can's tab with deft, practised movements, and he takes it from her and sets it on the tray table next to his.

Thank you, you say again, and you shift your daughter's weight to free a hand, and take the cup from him.

Cheers, he says, the twang of his accent making it almost two syllables, like yours, and you reply with your almost-two syllables, cheers, and you touch cups and sip.

To sleeping babies, he says, and you say, Look, I'm so sorry, and he says, I once flew solo with the twins when they'd just turned three, Vancouver to Sydney, with a layover in LA, oh boy.

Solo with twins, you say, and he says, Yeah, my wife was away and the childminder was sick, it was like a bad farce, I wouldn't wish that journey on anyone, and he's quiet for a moment and says, My sister died an hour before we got there, and then he says, Sorry.

My cousin just died, you say, and I hadn't seen her in years, but for a while she was like a sister to me.

I'm sorry, he says, at the same time you say, Sorry, too, because a cousin you haven't spoken to in years is not the same as a sister, and even if there's no real metric to grief, there is, must be, a hierarchy of loss.

You touch cups again, sombrely this time, and sip, and finally break eye contact and look away, and neither of you says anything for a while, until he says, That's twenty years ago now, and you say nothing, because what is there to say?

The blazing sunshine and high blue skies, t-shirt weather, the leaves just turning on the trees, a stupidly perfect day. The cool and calm of the mortuary chapel, old for Toronto, designed and built, you read, by John G. Howard in 1842. White brick and Georgetown stone, deep-set trefoil windows and the steeply pitched roof; a fine example of Gothic Revival architecture in Canada. In the little vestibule, the tinny bluegrass of *Hey Duggee* from your phone as the Squirrels arrived again and again at the Clubhouse to bake carrot cakes for the stoner bunnies; Roly, the excitable little hippo, and Happy, the crocodile with his adoptive elephant parents, Betty the octopus rocking up in her dad's little orange submarine, Norrie the mouse and Tag the rhino, all leaping up, to Tilly's delight, for their Duggee-hug; while in the nave the priest intoned and the mourners responded, standing and sitting and singing and weeping, and your cousin was no more.

We are all ashes and dust eventually, you think, but now she already was: her warm taut body, pressed next to yours in your sleeping bags zipped together, as she confided about a boy she'd kissed; her long brown legs in their blue shorts with the red piping taking the stairs two and three at a time, the tattoos she tried to give you both when you were twelve and she was fourteen with the spike of her compass and a cartridge of ink from your yellow Parker fountain pen, below your hipbone where neither of your mothers would see it, and where a smudge of blue dots still remains.

You think of all of this and you think how impossible it is that all of it's gone; how the fact of its being gone makes none of it, nothing, feel true any more, not that people can ever really know each other, or truly love, or that it matters in the end if a marriage fails, or ever could have worked; and yet how can it all not matter?

The meals trolley has made its way to you. Your tray table doesn't fold down over your daughter's sleeping body, so he takes your meal on his too, arranges both little trays lengthwise.

Shall I cut it up for you? he says, and you laugh in embarrassment as he tears and butters your bread roll, forks up cubes of chicken, the way you might for Tilly.

You don't manage more than a few bites before it all becomes too much – the bizarre intimacy of this stranger feeding you.

I'm fine, you say, I'm actually not that hungry, and it's true, you haven't been for a while, and not just because of the jet lag, or since the initial shock of your cousin's death, but for weeks now, maybe even months. You know you're getting thin, and you've brushed it off and blamed it on running after a toddler, and you've made an effort, for her as much as for you, to make yourself eat. But the hollow feeling at your centre, the ache in your solar plexus, voids all hunger, and it feels somehow right to be at a light-headed remove from the world, this sense of being vague, and insubstantial, as if you could just drift on, indefinitely; as if you don't really exist, or need to. Sometimes, you think, your daughter is the only person who feels real, because the immediacy of her needs is so urgently, incontrovertibly so.

So what do you do, he's saying, as if he's reading your mind, or are you a full-time mom? and you're saying, No, I'm an architect, then qualifying it with, at least I used to be, because what, actually, do you do now with your days, beyond endlessly push a buggy round the city streets, taking photographs, not even with your SLR, just screens' and screens' worth of photos on your phone, stone detailing or glazed-brick facades, ghost signage or board-marked concrete, large Queen Anne sash windows or tiny Huguenot busts to hold shutters in place, not even for any reason, you've even stopped bothering to upload them to your laptop any more.

From November, you say, when Tilly turns two, you'll have the nursery place: three mornings a week to begin with, then when she settles, the afternoon sessions too. Your husband says you should take on some private resi. Leaflet the neighbours. Loft conversions or extensions, something to keep you busy, get you working again. He's begun to say lately that you could set up your own practice, as if he doesn't know the first thing about architecture, despite being married to you all these years. But at the same time he's sort of right: what else are you going to do with your days?

He nods, listening, and you find yourself talking on.

Another baby would of course be the logical thing, and as an only child yourself, you badly want Tilly to have a brother or sister; and yet. Every time you have the discussion, about babies, or work, about what happens next, you feel deeply tired; an exhaustion that seeps into, or maybe from, your very bones. Bone-weary: you used to feel a sort of delight when a word or a phrase was a perfect fit, the mathematical logic of it; but now, for the first time in your life, you just feel old.

You stop, abruptly, expecting him to laugh at that, but he doesn't laugh.

I'm fifty-six, he says, which on a bad day rounds up to sixty, and I'm two years divorced, and my boys are almost twenty-four.

You realise you've been trying to work out his age.

Fifty-six, you say, not meaning to say it aloud, and he puts up his hands and winces.

I'm not, he says, I know I'm not, but in so many ways I still feel twenty-four myself.

I know what you mean, you say. I mean, I don't feel any different, I don't think, than I did then?

I don't think, he says, we ever really do.

You don't think people change, you say, or ever really can?

I think people change, he says, for sure, but only ever become, essentially, more themselves.

You don't know if that thought is comforting or profoundly sad.

Then where's the hope, you say, if we can never truly begin again, or become, I don't know, something else or better?

He shrugs, and smiles. Each moment, I guess, he says. Each moment, here now, that's what we have.

That's what we have, or that's all we have?

Perhaps it's both.

A girl you were at university with had married a man twenty-five years older, more, technically, than twice her age: she twenty-four, he forty-nine. She'd been engaged before that to a guy from uni; he'd been a Blue and they were something of a golden couple. No one could understand it. You didn't know her very well, but you somehow once got drunk together and she started crying and said the loneliest

thing in the world was lying in bed with someone and wanting someone else's hands to be on you instead.

They had a daughter whom they'd had almost immediately, long before any of your other uni friends had kids, who
must be in her teens by now. After that drunken night you'd
stayed in touch for a while, and bought a present when the
baby was born, a ruffled pinafore from a place whose clothes
cost as much as adult clothes, and came, in a sort of performance by the cashier, wrapped in palest lemon tissue.

That was the only time you'd been to their house, because
you felt so awkward there. They had peonies in vases, and Le
Creuset pans, and a magnetic knife rack with proper, mono-
grammed knives, and different-sized wine glasses for white
or red, and acres of white linen on the huge bed you passed
on the way to the baby's room, and the guest bathroom, with
its cut-grass scented soap. The house, in retrospect, wasn't
that remarkable – just a modest terrace on a street in Kentish
Town – but it felt at the time like being at someone's posh
English parents', and you'd thought how strange it was that
this, now, was her life, a quantum leap away from bedsits and
flatshares and badly carved-up Victorian houses and boxy
shared-ownership starter flats.

But what struck and maybe discomfited you most was
how devoted she was to him: as if, after all they'd done,
there wasn't the luxury of being anything else – exasper-
ated, or bickering. It had seemed to you an exhausting way
of living; although you wonder now if maybe it wasn't that
at all, but rather the knowledge that they'd found each
other too late in life, or in his life at least, to be reckless, or

casual; that the way they loved was careful and tender not because they didn't, but because they did love each other with a sort of abandon.

You have Riedel wine glasses and Dartington Crystal champagne flutes yourself now, and Japanese knives and a proper knife-sharpener, and sometimes even peonies in vases, or at least in a vase. Where has it all come from? How have you graduated, almost without noticing, from novelty shot glasses and wine glasses nicked from pubs, thick-rimmed and engraved with measures, to this? How have you come so far from your Pioneer parents, their bottle of Shloer at Christmastime or weddings, the single blue bottle of Harveys Bristol Cream they kept as a concession to your grandma? A wedding of your own; a marriage to a producer with extravagant Christmas and birthday and anniversary tastes. And yet: you can't shake the sense that it has all crept up on you without your wanting or asking for it, without your feeling any different than you did at twenty-nine, twenty-seven, or, yes, twenty-four.

Can I ask you something? he says, and you say, inexplicably flustered, Sure.

He picks up the book, which has fallen to the floor, and opens it.

Do you really believe in – well, that? he says. That people are mean, and bad, and – for want of a better word – damned?

He looks at the mean and bad people for a moment

before closing the book and reaching to slide it back into your tote bag.

I was brought up believing it all, you say. God and Noah, the Flood, the Ark – I was brought up believing it was literal truth. That the world was six thousand years old and the Devil had planted fossils to try to trick us.

So that sounds like you no longer believe it.

Your aunty: pale-faced, her hair drawn back to show new cheekbones, gaunt, but lit with the belief that your cousin was finally in a better place. The way the priest talked about the prescription drugs as her demons. The flights of angels that would have been there for her at the end.

I sometimes think it would be easier if I still did.

That's why you read it to your daughter?

Oh no, you say. No! I'm not – I'm going to tactically misplace the book as soon as we get home. My aunty just gave it to her. It's something to read – that's all.

I guess I'd like to think, he says, that people are basically good.

Neither of you says anything for a while.

I'd love to be able to live like that, you say, and just for a moment it feels like a weight is lifting.

Your daughter wakes. Her ears are sore, and she doesn't understand it. You've used your last carton of milk. He goes to the galley and comes back with a handful of UHT sticks which he tears and empties, one by one, into her bottle, the millilitres accumulating until there's enough for her to drink. While he does this, you pace with her, joggle her, up and down the cabin, and although the lights are dimmed now and most people are sleeping, or attempting to, no one looks at you angrily. When the bottle is filled enough, he holds Tilly while you go to the loo. In the little metal room, you splash water on your face and think: I must do better. I must start eating again, and make a plan for what happens next.

Even when Tilly sleeps again, you don't, and nor does he. You both watch the minute, ticking progress of the little blue plane icon, over the emptiness of the North Atlantic Ocean, its route curving up towards Greenland and the Labrador Sea before it will begin to fall again towards Ireland and onwards and home, endless, inexorable. You watch it, and talk some more, and these are some of the things you talk about. How unfeasible it is that this great sleek lumbering mass of metal can rise instead of falling, into the sky, up and up, can traverse the globe along invisible, predetermined tracks, corridors in the air, while its passengers sleep and watch films and flush toilets and request more ice for their gin and tonic and eat bread rolls specially engineered to taste normal at low pressure and in dry cabin air. That there is the world, the ocean, the dark roiling waves, thirty-however-many thousand feet beneath, and here you are, suspended above it all, hurtling onwards at hundreds of miles an hour into the dawn of an entirely different day. How time as a measure is, for a while, entirely meaningless, in this time out of time, and how distance is too, and about the distances we travel, between where we come from and where we end up, between who we thought we were and who we turn out to be. About how – who knows? – for your daughter there will not be transatlantic travel, at least not like this, and it may seem the most grotesque decadence of a bygone age. We think, or rather we live – or at least you do, or have – as if things will continue forever, and we so rarely talk about the only things, in hindsight, that matter. All of these words, these thousands of words, and none of them the right ones, the handful of words that might have meant or even changed something. And, once again, only this time with even more urgency, *can* people change, or is it already too late, is it always too late? Or is there always another brief window in which anything is possible?

And these are just some of the things.

The plane descends. Tray tables and seat backs, seat belts, final cabin checks. Blurs of light resolving themselves into constellated pinpoints; buildings, roads, almost individual headlamps. The rattle and grind of the landing gears, the final roar of the engines. The headlong rush of the plane onto tarmac, the shuddering certainty of it. Your stomach lurching.

He carries your bags for you off the plane as you carry Tilly, still heavy with sleep. You wait together as they fetch the buggy, and you kick and yank it upright, and strap Tilly in. By this stage, you're among the last off the plane, and several other red-eye flights have come in too, and the Immigration hall is packed.

Oh no, you say, and he rests a hand lightly on your shoulder.

Hello, Heathrow, my old friend.

For a moment, you stand there, in the crowd, breathing as one.

Sir, madam, this way, please, a uniformed woman is saying, families this way, and she's sliding open a barrier tape so that you can pass into the Family & Special Assistance lane.

He smiles at you, and you smile back.

Thank you, you say to the uniformed woman.

As you manoeuvre the buggy around and join the other lane, which doesn't seem to be moving any faster, perhaps even slower, he murmurs in your ear, Though whether this is a help or a disincentive for travelling as a family, time alone shall tell.

You pass through Immigration as a family, through Baggage Reclaim, and pause before the sliding doors of the Arrivals hall, where your husband will be meeting you and Tilly: he's timed his flight back from Cape Town to coincide with yours.

So I guess this is it, he says. Are you going to be ok?

Yes, you say, because what else can you possibly say?

And you take the handle of your suitcase from him, and you walk, not a family at all but two entirely separate people now, through the final Customs channel; *Nothing to Declare.*

Your husband isn't there.

You find a power socket and plug in your phone. A series of messages: he's been further delayed in Cape Town, the assistant producer couldn't handle it after all, the dancer who's broken her ankle, the problem with insurance, the sequence that needs to be reshot. He had to turn back halfway to the airport to deal with it all. He's not now going to be home until tomorrow, or maybe the next day, he won't know until tonight. He's going to make it up to you. Love to Tilly. Tell her he's got the biggest present for her. Take a cab!

You knew it, you thought. Even as he was texting you as you boarded the flight in Toronto, saying he was on his way to the airport too, you knew and dreaded this.

You hold down the button until your phone goes dark again.

He stays with the buggy and bags and the charging phone while you go, Tilly grizzling on your hip, to rinse out the bottle in a sink in the loos then beg some warm milk from the Costa. You could do with a coffee yourself, and should have offered to get him one, but you don't have enough hands. You think of your mother: her jokes about needing a spare pair of hands, her claim to have eyes in the back of

her head that you and your cousin once combed her hair
repeatedly to disprove. Your mother would have been
younger than you are now. You and your cousin just a
handful of years from your daughter.

It goes, all of it, and then it's just – gone.

But here you are, now. The chaotic, impatient bustle of
Heathrow Arrivals, all the milling, surging, purposeful,
harried people. Seven seventeen in the morning, a September Tuesday.

Tilly, strapped back in the buggy, draining her milk,
temporarily quiet.

Right, you say, and take the handle of your case again.
Ok.

Let me give you a lift, he says, there'll be a driver for me,
a car, I'll see you safely home.

His eyes are very blue.

For a moment, you almost say yes.

You think of the books that you and your cousin loved,
the ones with multiple pathways through, and dozens of
endings. You'd read them lying on your stomachs, heads
pressed together, holding various pages, options, open. You'd
always be careful, trying to make it through, and she'd choose
the most reckless routes possible, just to see what might happen. She would have gone with him. You think: If she was
still here, at the other end of a WhatsApp stream or the tap
of a FaceTime away, she'd say to you, Do it.

But no, you hear yourself saying, it will be easier with
your daughter on the train, she's been cooped up so long,
at least in a train you can walk up and down, and besides,

she gets carsick. The train to Paddington, then, and then the tube, and maybe a taxi for the last bit, at the very end. But your bags, and the buggy, he says, how will you manage?

People are helpful, you say, they've been so helpful, every bit of the way – and it's true, you realise in a rush, thinking of the taxi driver who found you a trolley, wheeled your bags into the terminal, right up to the Air Canada desk; of Chantal, who upgraded you to premium economy for free, so you and Tilly would have a bit more room. Her long nails, midnight-blue with crystals, tapping, and how, in an attempt to give her something back, you'd said how you admired them, offering up your own short, bitten fingernails, and how she'd beamed. Of the people around you who didn't roll their eyes or glare at you as Tilly howled; and him, of course; and him – and suddenly, you find yourself on the verge of all the tears you haven't yet cried.

Oh, he says, oh, and he says, Come here, and he takes your face in both his hands and brushes away the tears with his thumbs, and then there's a moment, and everything tilts.

Heathrow Arrivals resolves itself back around you. There is an artist whose work you saw once in a Whitechapel gallery: she had stitched to a globe of the world metallic threads representing one single day's flights, then somehow dissolved the globe, leaving just the sugar-spun mass of threads, and you think of it now, of how it made you think, how fine the threads that connect us from one person, or place, to another, and how precious, and how strong.

I have to go, you say, because if you stay for a moment longer, you won't; or won't be able to.

What are you going to do now? he says.

Now this minute now, or now in a more existential sense? you say, and somehow you manage to say it lightly.

He looks at you, then takes up your cue. Somewhere between the two?

We're going to watch *Hey Duggee* on the train, for as long as the battery lasts. We're going to be home by ten. We're going to press all the buttons in the lift. We're going to do the shopping and maybe bake a cake, which will really be a pretext for cracking lots of eggs and bashing the shells up with a teaspoon.

He laughs. You realise you love that laugh. You love that you've made him laugh. For a moment, nothing else matters.

Ok then, he says, softly, and you hear or maybe feel him take a breath, and let it slowly out. Take it easy.

Take it easy, you say back.

Ok, he says. Goodbye.

Goodbye, you say.

You do let Tilly press all of the buttons in the lift, all seven of them, from LG for the car park to the floors beyond your flat. You don't sigh when the slow doors judder open and closed, open and closed. You just feel numb. You do bake the cake. You let Tilly crack the whole carton of eggs, far more than you need, and you think it's ok, you'll make an omelette later. You tell her the joke about Hamlet and egos that your cousin, at thirteen, had to explain to you; and you turn away before she can see that your laughter at how clever you thought it is turning to sobs.

From your little balcony, the September sky is high and cloudless.

You could email him, you think. You didn't swap addresses, but you could google his name, his company. You won't, but you could.

You call up a Google tab on your phone.

You won't. You don't.

You look at a map of Canada on your phone instead. It's so vast, is what gets you, there's just so much *space*; the cities of Toronto and Ottawa and Montreal and then Quebec City in a tidy row just up from New York state and the US border; and above them the open space of Ontario and Quebec and Newfoundland and Labrador; and westwards beyond that the breadth of Manitoba and Saskatchewan and British Columbia; Vancouver, where he was born and lived for the two and a half decades of his marriage, and northwards of it the Yukon and the Northwest Territories and Nunavut, the whole sweep of it, so empty, so much, that you have to hold on to the balustrade to steady yourself, on the verge of doubling over with a sort of homesickness, this sudden intensity of loss.

Breathe, you tell yourself, just breathe.

Your husband is only doing his best. He's been so worried, since Tilly was born, and you stopped work, about providing for you; about the precariousness of his industry; about what it means to be a family. He's doing his best and you think that you must do your best too, to still love him, and you think that love gone wrong or astray is also a kind of exile.

It was right, you tell yourself, not to accept the lift. It would have been a line crossed; some new frontier, new country, from which you might not have returned.

And yet.

You wonder, can't help yourself wondering, what it would have been like had you gone with him: in his executive car, even back to his hotel, maybe, where he holds you in his arms; kneels before you and presses his face to you; eases your jeans from your hips and unbuttons your shirt and lays you carefully on his bed; and maybe that's what you want, for someone to undress you and lay you down, to make the decisions for you; but however you try to stage the sequence in your head, you can't get past the fact of your daughter there, and the whole thing dissipates.

You try to keep Tilly up until her bedtime, but she's far too tired, and so you give in mid-afternoon. It means she'll be wide awake at midnight, but so, probably, will you. She wants the book, which you have forgotten to lose, but you barely begin it before she's sucking the collar of your lumberjack shirt and has fallen asleep. You lie there for a while before attempting to ease her down, gazing at the cartoon people with their ugly, gargoyle faces. *All the people were mean and bad*, except that what he said is right – they weren't, they couldn't be, that isn't the way you want to live this life, or whatever of it remains to you. They were only doing their best, you think, or the best they thought they could; and unlike stern, righteous, virtuous Noah, no one, ever, told them they were going to die, or be saved, or that any of it, in the end, ever mattered.

Devotions

THE THREAT OF SNOW HAS YOU ON THE ROAD the night before you'd intended to leave. The cottage hunkers down against a steep rise, accessible only across two sheep-strewn fields, and any downfall will leave it cut off.

That morning, a barn owl swooped at you from an abandoned dwelling on the dale, its pale round face and curved wingspan, before soaring upwards and away, leaving your hearts skittering. You peered in through the empty gaps where windows should be, lifting the older boys on your shoulders so they could see in too. The floorboards were rotting but the outer structure was solid, the old cast-iron gutters still sound, and for a moment you imagined living there, stepping out of this house into the morning light, the ancient hawthorns bent into supplicating shapes by the wind streaming cold and pure.

The barn owl's cry, you read in a book back at the cottage, once heralded imminent death; this inhabitant of profane and lonely places. A screeching owl in daylight was indeed a harbinger of snow; or else a witch come to suck a baby's blood. But it had seemed, at the time, less a warning than some strange blessing.

You loaded the car and set the satnav: the thin, twisting roads through the dales that would become carriageways then motorways, as if impelled by the journey's own momentum. Driving up, on Boxing Day, you'd been amused by the road signs heralding *The North*, as if it were a place rather than a concept, something not relative, but real. You missed your own North, then, and your once-ritual walk round the deserted, expectant city-centre streets on Christmas Eve morning; the lingering skies of a city salved from sleech, and ruled by water. At the unlikeliest times you felt the tug of it, like the twitch of a dowsing rod. You'd never imagined you'd be calling London's grimy East End *home*.

You said your goodbyes, shivering in the frosty air, the cousins milling and jostling in a pack of skinny limbs, then strapped in the children, wearing cardigans over their pyjamas, the boy with his neck-pillow shaped like an elephant, the baby in her backwards-facing carrier. It was just gone six; the satnav said you should be home by midnight. The sky glittered with stars. It felt later than it was by hours, years. The light you saw now had left the stars aeons ago, long before you, before any of this. You pulled the car doors shut and waved, the others briefly silhouetted in the orange square of light between wide flagstones and heavy lintel, before the field dipped and the car lurched and they too dropped out of sight.

The snow began to fall on the outskirts of Doncaster, as the A1(M) became the A1 and then the M18, the first signs for *The South* somehow less beguiling. Past Sheffield and Chesterfield and Nottingham and Grantham, the heartlands of this country you barely know at all. Birmingham is the Midlands, and Peterborough the hinge between north and south, but despite your years here you would struggle to place them on a map. The voice of the satnav, set, half as a joke, to a Northern Irish accent. The accent, in places, is meant to be as close as English gets to the way that Shakespeare spoke it: the quirks and rhythms of the Planters, the Tudor noblemen given swathes of land, forbidden from marrying or even employing the dispossessed, preserved in certain pockets for centuries. *Continue straight ahead.*

The children, who had fallen asleep soon after the journey began, slept on as the miles unrolled. The little blue arrow creeping blindly along its preordained line.

Music, then no music. Talking, then slipping into silence. The intimacy of driving at night, outside of time. Long journeys of your childhood coming back to you. Coming back over the Glenshane Pass, after holidays in Donegal. The yellow grass of the blanket bog, slashed dark brown when you passed peat workings. The scree slopes tumbling down the highest of the Sperrin Mountains. Coming back from Ayrshire, the slow, familiar roads to Stranraer; the briny smell of diesel in the ferry's bowels; keeping your balance on the slimy, salty deck as it stubbornly shunted its way across the Irish Sea and into the mouth of the lough;

piling into the car again, the gangway heaving and clanging open, and those final miles home, wanting to be back, not wanting the journey to end.

You were struck, as you often are these days, by how little, if anything, the children would remember of this. The baby nothing at all, and even the boy almost nothing, unless it became a family story. Remember the time we stayed with your cousins in Yorkshire and a barn owl swooped down on us in the day? And yet, you thought, it must all be there, somewhere, however inaccessible it later would be.

Your husband lowered and raised the window: a sudden blast of cold air, the buffeting roar in your ears. He was white-faced with tiredness and you felt with a deep rush your love for him. You unwrapped a chocolate coin, plunder from your son's Christmas stocking, and put it in his mouth, then one for yourself, the cheap, grainy, metallic taste of it, and you forced yourself to sit up straight, to stay awake, to keep your own eyes focused, through the hypnotic swirls of snowflakes, as if the strength of your attention might keep you all safe on the road.

The closer you get to home, the slower the roads are, the last couple of miles done at a crawl. There is no snow in London, just the dank residue of slush against the kerbs. Bin bags and cardboard boxes piled up on the pavements, already the occasional yellowing Christmas tree. Through Poplar and the East India Docks. Limehouse and Stepney on the Commercial Road, once Orchard Lane, then a brickfield; earlier than that, a series of the East End's deepest plague pits. Public houses and stables, market gardens and music halls. The Blitz. A scrappy park frequented by local alcoholics and flocks of belligerent pigeons, named after a young Sylheti clothing worker stabbed to death. Syringes among the ancient, weathered slabs of gravestone in the corner by the takeaway's extractor fans.

Home, you think; a Zeno's paradox. Motion is impossible and change an illusion. The arrow is neither moving to where it is, nor where it is not, and therefore St Sebastian never died. Zeno of Elea, Plato and his cave, Aristotle, Socrates with his cup of hemlock. The years you spent studying them, trying to shape your mind to think like them. Lately, all they said seems meaningless, or at least irrelevant. Now you wonder if they ever gazed at a newborn's face and felt the world tilt and fall away; watched a child grow up and felt the panic of time. Motion is not impossible: in fact the opposite. Life rushes by, streams through the attempt to snatch at it, then suddenly parts to show you glimpses of the next world, and the next, the ceaseless change to come.

In the underground car park, you sit with the children asleep as your husband takes the bags up, turns on the heating, makes a hot-water bottle for your son's bed underneath the draughty window. These offerings, these devotions, banal and endless, our days going round and rushing from under us; the measure of our love.

When your husband returns, he takes the baby-carrier and the final bag and you unbuckle and lift your son, the surprising weight of him, nudging his arms around your neck and his legs around your waist, and he murmurs and nuzzles at you. It seems impossible that *here you are*, a mother with children, a family of four. All the people you've been, or imagined being. All the people you've known, and loved, and love. There are times in your life you would have looked with bewilderment at this; at other times you would, with astonishment, have said, Yes, I'll take that. Yes.

Through the car park, its low ceiling and flickering lights and smell of damp, and slowly up the stairs, four, five flights of them, pausing on each landing. Then into the flat, the ticking of the radiators and clanking of reluctant pipes, and sleepwalking your son to the toilet, holding his hips as he grumbles and aims. Unbuttoning his cardigan, wriggling the final wooden toggle through its too-tight buttonhole. The cardy was knitted by your mother, wool chosen and bought on the Lower New-townards Road, buttons from the box of buttons you loved as a child, running your fingers through the cool slippery mass of them, selecting a single one and closing your hand around it tight. You think, now, that it's a kind of spell, the knitting of a garment for a loved one; each stitch a ravelling-up to keep them safe. You fold and put the cardy on a chair, still heavy with the warmth of him, and hug him one last time then tuck him into bed. Is this my bed, Mummy? *Shh*, it is, yes. Good, let's never, ever leave, promise me, Mummy, promise me we won't? And what can you say to that but, *Shh*, I love you, it's all ok, and everything will be ok, I love you, *shh*.

The baby has woken and is crying now, and your husband is changing her nappy and attempting to soothe her too, shushing and singing and turning the mobile above her changing mat, but the pitch of her cry is rising and all she wants is you. This burden, this privilege. You take her into your bed and she latches on and feeds in desperation before finally lolling, open-mouthed, asleep. You ease her onto your chest, the way you held her as a newborn, so she could hear the sound of your heart. Already she's getting too big for this. You can feel the outwards rise of her ribcage with each breath, as it presses against yours. You think you'll never forget the particular weight of them, and then you do, and another's newborn is terrifyingly flimsy and insubstantial, as if, though you try not even to think it, they haven't yet committed to the world. The way you and your husband, on your first trip as a new family into town, could barely contain your giggles at the sight of two toddlers in buggies in a lift, such swollen and overgrown babies, alongside your perfectly sized firstborn in his bassinet.

You go to text your husband the memory but you've left your phone, you realise, in the car, in the cavity in the door on the passenger side. You almost go to text him to tell him that you've left it there and can he—

Instead, you close your eyes and listen to him in the room next door, singing to your son, the songs your son loves, dragons and flowers and grandfather clocks; all, ultimately, about loss, which is maybe why you sing them: to inoculate, to prepare, for the time you won't be there and he'll know nothing of how much you loved him, the quotidian task and blessing of it. Do you remember the owl?

The dales seem a lifetime away. Just this morning, clambering up to see the ponds brimming with winter rain, the blank trees around them not yet even imagining their leaves. Your son, after a brave attempt to keep up with his cousins, wanting to be carried. Come back next summer, they'd said, and we can have picnics on the ridge. For a moment you see your son, brown-legged and golden-haired, scrambling ahead, racing joyfully away from you. Maybe the baby too would be walking by then.

The warm heft of her on your chest. Those lines by Keats come into your head, the sonnet at the very end of the battered A-level textbook, which was also, maybe, the last poem he ever wrote. Pillowed forever upon my sweet love's breast. No: that's not quite it, but you can't check now, so you let it pass. Nature's sleepless eremite. You remember the volta of that poem. But what if eternity does not mean endless time, but an escape from it? What if, from the perspective of eternity, time is a droplet, held together by its own surface tension, everything that had happened, or ever would, taking place simultaneously, and already over?

You think, then, of the children who flickered only so

briefly in your body and in your mind; never met, never kissed, never held; yet held somewhere in the unfathomable depths and reach of love.

The lives unlived; the loves yet not unloved.

We get to choose, in this life, what is most holy, and we must do our best to honour it.

The snow upon the mountains and the moors.

The baby's breathing. This. This. This.

Intimacies

i

IMAGINE THIS. I am at an airport, flying somewhere with your brother – or trying to; for some reason flights are delayed and all is chaos. Your brother is not yet your brother, nor yet, in any tangible sense, are you *you*, though I sometimes seem to catch glimpses of you, at the edge of my mind as I'm falling asleep, or a moment before waking. The tannoy has just announced that our flight is, in fact, boarding now, at a gate a shuttle ride and fifteen minutes away. Your brother hasn't napped and I haven't eaten; I am attempting to hold him on my hip with one arm as he wriggles and cries, as I push the buggy precariously balanced with our bags, negotiating the queue in the sandwich bar. It's finally our turn and the cashier calls me forward. As she starts to ask what coffee I want, a tanned, besuited businessman, all cufflinks and expensive watch, steps up and says, It was quite obviously my turn next and you pushed right in front of me.

I hadn't – or maybe I had, but hadn't entirely meant to

– and, spurred on by the look of disdain on the cashier's face, I turned to face him in a burst of self-righteousness, unleashing a tirade that went something like this. Even if it had been his turn next, even if I had deliberately cut in front of him, even if his flight was boarding right now as mine was, perhaps he should see where a little compassion got him, because however in the right he no doubt felt he was, you can never know what's going on in someone else's head or heart and maybe your behaviour is going to make or break them, or at least their day. Try it, I blazed, just try some compassion and see where it gets you in life.

I should say, at this point, that this was two days after we'd lost you, or lost the baby we thought would be you. A clot of cells far smaller than the weeks we thought you were, no heartbeat, no more than twenty minutes in the operating theatre and home by lunch. But yet.

The businessman shot his cuffs and puffed his chest and smirked. I'm doing pretty well in life, thanks, and I flashed back: I'm talking about your spiritual life, and it was momentarily glorious.

Five minutes later, I thought: Oh.

What if the whole point of my being there, in that queue, on that day, late and flustered and aching with grief, is that it was *my* chance to show compassion?

Because of course it was, and I failed.

And what if it's even more than that? What if the whole of my life, everything I'd done and been, the places I'd gone, the people I'd known, had led up to that: this one, petty, banal-seeming moment which held within it the possibility of transformation? And instead I gloried in how superior it felt to be so in the right. What if, as I asked myself then and have done almost daily since, what if the people we dislike the most, long standing nemeses to fleeting antagonists, are those that love us most, that love us so much they have chosen to bear our anger, scorn, contempt? We think the tests will come on the days we're ready for them, braced and prepared, but they don't: they come to us unheralded, unexpected, in disguise, the ordinariest of moments.

That's the first thing I'd tell you.

ii

People daubing ochre onto subterranean walls. Placing a spread palm on the stone and blowing pigment round to leave their hand's outline. Carving a reindeer's antler into a pipe that plays three rising notes. Leaving the cave with smudges on their lips and wrists and foreheads, climbing variously solemn and laughing into the light. This day, this moment, we were here: us. That handful of notes vibrating on, long after it ceases to be audible, the pattern of the outwards air forever altered.

You were born in the grip of a heatwave. All across England, in Ireland too, the sun-scorched land gave up its secrets: the outline of an Iron Age fort, and a Victorian ghost garden; a medieval castle and a World War II airfield. On the radio, they explained these landscape scars: crop marks, they are called, and they appear when plants absorb water and nutrients from the ditches where fortifications once stood. I read too that time doesn't heal wounds – or that it does, but it can also unheal them. A lack of vitamin C means the body's collagen stores deplete, and old scars resurface and reopen. At sea, sailors in the grip of scurvy would find themselves dying of old, surmounted wounds and childhood injuries considered overcome. I lay on the bed as your brother napped beside me, the rise and fall of his chest, his damp flushed cheeks, the murmur of the radio, thinking of this, of things unknown and known.

As the weeks went on and the waters receded, scientists discovered footsteps on an estuary shore dating back three quarters of a million years. They could, impossible as it seemed, deduce that a woman had walked that way, a healthy woman of about twenty years old and standing one and a half metres tall. Three, or possibly four, children aged between two and eight had walked with her; at one point, she probably carried the youngest. They would have walked northwards across the wet mud, through brackish water, in a climate that was more akin to modern-day Sweden than the east of England today, with cool, mild summers and brutal winters, in search of shellfish and edible plants. The river valley where they walked would have been grazed by woolly mammoths, hippos, a sort of proto-rhinoceros. As they walked, the heels of their feet and then their toes sinking into the mud, a quirk of tides and sand and sedimentation preserved their footprints for all these centuries, millennia, until the summer they briefly appeared and, in the act of appearing, vanished.

That is the second thing.

iii

The third is that lately I've been rereading Winnicott: his *good-enough* mother is everywhere, as some things are when we most need to hear them. *What you do and know*, he says, to his imaginary young mother, *simply by virtue of the fact that you are the mother of an infant, is as far apart from what you know by learning as is the east from the west coast of England. I cannot put this too strongly*, he says. *Just as the professor who found out about the vitamins that prevent rickets really has something to teach you, so you really have something to teach him about the other kind of knowledge, that which comes to you naturally.* We know, I tell myself. Sometimes we forget we know, or mistrust that we do, but we do know.

There is so much we need to learn, and you are here to teach me too, and we learn together.

But deep inside, we know.

We understand so little of love, and we let fear get in the way: fear that we won't be good enough, or that we're not ready, or that we'll fuck it up. Fear that we won't love well, or maybe enough. As I grew you in my body, so too I grew you in my mind; that latter task no less important, a turning inwards, a kind of vigil, the dark art of imagining you into being. When you were born, of course, you confounded all

expectations; withheld yourself; so simply *were* that for the
first hours and first few days all I could say to your father,
in a kind of bewilderment edged with panic, was that I
didn't know you. Until, imperceptibly and then all at once,
something shifted, and you were just you.

iv

I wish I could tell you my struggles, in a way that would be
meaningful or even of some practical use. But the secret,
most important battles we fight are almost untranslatable
to anyone else; and besides, you'll have your own seething
weirs of tigerish waters to cross.

I repeat to myself daily that every day, every moment of
each day, is a chance to respond to the world with love, not
fear. That fear is not an equal and opposing force, but rather
the absence of love, a symptom or signal of something
askew or astray. But I am terrified of making the wrong
choices. Of doing the wrong thing. I am terrified of getting in the way of your life. I mark the margin of Kate
Chopin's *The Awakening* where Edna Pontellier says: I
would give my money, I would give my life for my children; but I wouldn't give myself. I don't dare ask myself, or
maybe the better verb is answer, if it's true.

V

This summer, I've been obsessed with Françoise Gilot, an artist who fell in love with Picasso. She was twenty-one when they met, to his sixty-one; they lived together for almost a decade, had two children. She remains, the story goes, the only woman ever to walk away from him: and it is this, her leaving, that has obsessed me.

After leaving him she wrote a memoir, a *succès de scandale*, which review upon review branded a fascinating insight into living with a genius, and crucial to our understanding of him, but which seems, to me, to be her own self-portrait; her way of figuring out where he ends and she begins. The reviewers reeled off breathless lists of Giacometti and Gide, Chagall and Chaplin, Cocteau, Hemingway, Matisse, the flamboyant characters who populate her book, but reading it, all I can see is her, her seeing them, and the rising knowledge that she was going to, would have to, leave him, that world, behind.

The memoir's recently been reprinted and to mark the occasion, she gave an interview to a journalist from the *New York Times*. She'd been impatient, spiky. Why, she said, should I look back twice? Regret is for something you have not done. You have to be true to yourself, and only then, if there's time, can you be true to others.

I look at the photo of her on the inner back cover: ninety-seven now, head slightly tilted and entirely poised, sleek black hair side-parted with a tortoiseshell clip, lips half-smiling, eyes candid and luminous and grave. But it is her hands that make the picture. She holds them up in front of her, pale and broad and thickly veined, left hand over right, forefinger just touching her throat. It is a careful pose, and an utterly vulnerable one. I look at it and think of Françoise at thirty, at twenty-one. Her respectable, upper-middle-class parents, who'd sent her to Cambridge and to the Sorbonne, expecting she'd become a lawyer. Her own children, barred, in his rage, from seeing their father after she left. The friends and the critics who closed ranks and condemned her. The public outcry and the outrage and the scathing prurience. Her necessary brusqueness: Why should I be afraid?

There is a painting of her infant daughter asleep in her crib that I gaze and gaze at. It's got the Picasso style of deconstructed form, the child's limbs flung akimbo, but it's somehow much softer, less angular, than his cubism. The child's face is perfect – the almost-flickering eyelids, pouted lips: you can see in it the love and fear and devotion of the young mother watching.

I watch you as you sleep, and I write this in my head, thinking of all the times in your life when you'll have to leave, someone or something or somewhere, but most of all someone. I think of the times I've had to leave, and leave again. I think of how much of life is rehearsals for departure. I think of Françoise, and I think of those words of Maya Angelou's: that when someone shows you who they are, believe them the first time. Picasso in the restaurant with his partner, Dora Maar, walking the few steps over to where Françoise was sitting to offer her a cherry from his bowl. The fifth thing I'd tell you: I wish you godspeed, in all those times to come.

vi

In a room not far from this room, now, in which I write, I told a man to close his eyes. I unbuttoned his shirt, all seven buttons, and then each cuff, and eased it from his shoulders and let it fall. I undid his trousers, the clasp and button and zip, eased them off too, and helped him step from them. When he was fully naked, I untied the halter of my dress and stepped from it. I raised his arms in the air and lifted the dress and slipped it over his arms onto him, the fluid silk soundless as it fell to the ground, and I stepped behind him and tied the ribbon straps around his neck. I could feel his quickened breath, his heart, as if it were my own. I walked a few steps from him, then stood. Open your eyes and walk to me, I said, and he did, and he did; and I understood something I hadn't before about desire.

Find someone, I would tell you, to whom you can say all the things you can never say. Look: I can make two people walk into a room, and have them do things to each other of which they may or may not have dreamed. I can make time run backwards, or take a different course entirely. I can summon the dead. It is a terrible kind of sorcery, and one I would not bequeath to you. That's the sixth thing. Art as merely a surfeit of desire, these words the currency of unspent love.

vii

And now the seventh, final thing, the most banal and profound of all. Tell the people you love that you love them. It will be the only thing, in the end, that counts for anything; the only thing we can take with us. Say it, now. Those small, quotidian, transfiguring words.

I wonder how old you'll be when you read this, and if I'll be gone, and of the dark magic that there is after all a way of telling you this, of putting it somewhere so that one day, when you need it, you might understand

That time is just a summary of time: everything's forever, and nothing is lost

That somehow our souls remember, and they rise in our bodies to tell us

That here I am

This private place achieved against the public odds; achieved and in a sense guaranteed because of them

Intimacies, first used in printed English in 1641, along with *catafalque, charism, eavesdropping*; along with *holy of holies, infinitude, intertwine*; with *jubilate, tantamount, tantivy, unfurl*

I give you these words and all of the words

Intimacies

All the words you'll live and the people you'll love and the places you'll go

Love being a holding-close and simultaneously a letting-go

All things, everything, at once

Now is always; and this a spell by which I've made it so.

Acknowledgements

I am very grateful to the Society of Authors for the K Blundell Trust Award, which enabled me to begin this collection, and will ever be to the Seamus Heaney Centre at Queen's University, Belfast, for the Fellowship during which the final stories were written.

My thanks to my first reader, Joe Thomas, and our book club (or valiant attempt thereat) of two plus occasional half. My agent, Peter Straus, of whose support I'm so profoundly glad, and my editor, Angus Cargill, with whom it's a joy and a privilege to work and from whom I've learned so much.

Thank you to everyone else at Faber who has helped to make this collection, including Libby Marshall, Josephine Salverda, Josh Smith and Jack Smyth, and to Silvia Crompton for her dark arts of copyediting. Also to Sarah Cleave, Sinéad Gleeson, Ra Page, Michael Shannon, David Torrans and Emma Warnock for their contributions to individually published stories.

My constant gratitude to my parents and sisters, Maureen, Peter, Kim and Faye Caldwell.

And finally, my thanks to my Tom, and William, and our brilliant force-for-good girl Orla. This collection is dedicated to her, and it's also especially for all London (particularly Northern) Irish.